Markus von Friedland

𝕮 𝖍 𝖗 𝖎 𝖘 𝖙 :

𝖂𝖍𝖆𝖙 𝖍𝖆𝖕𝖕𝖊𝖓𝖊𝖉   𝖆 𝖋 𝖙 𝖊 𝖗   𝕲𝖔𝖑𝖌𝖔𝖙𝖍𝖆 ??

An Introduction and Briefing to the following books:

1) The epic story of Christ in three volumes
based on the historic truth

2) Christ
The scientific proofs

Publications Andrômeda, Zurich, 2006

I N D E X

1. The explanation of the Cover-puzzle

a) The Roman arch under which Christ was presented by Pontius Pilate (Ecce homo)

b) Out of a biblical fragment of parchment the genuine mortuary mask of Jesus Christ glares over to us out of a distance of 20 centuries, in a tempestous-redish evening sky

c) Below this picture the ancient hebrew text: Father, they will be done

d) The mortuary mask of Jesus:

It is the tri-dimensional effigy of Christ's facial traits, extracted by the means of computer-tomography during two years of work by the italian professor G. Tamburelli, Turin, from the Holy Shroud of Turin, and cleaned from injuries caused by torture that had led to swellings and distortions. This picture was published in Italy only, in the magazine 'La Famiglia Cattolica, at Easter 1985 and represents the best image of Christ's physiognomy that has ever been obtained until this day.

The bushy eyebrows seem to signal the capability of anger in his character (see some Gospel-hints), the long nose tells of a tall stature (1,83 m) according to the measurements in the Holy Shroud, the soft traits around the mouth appear to indicate non-violence and compassion ('one never saw him laugh, but often cry', as a contemporary report would have it). The whole expression tells of dignity, eclecticisme, unapprochability, high intelligence and inward emotionallity. All comments of our gospel-authors do perfectly match this description.

He used to preceed the group of his disciples, who followed him at a distance of respect, we are told. - Christ's facial traits could not comply better with his most famous prayer, the 'Pater Noster'.

e) The Chorus-line of angels in the evening sky, celebrating Christ's elevation.

f) The tumblin cross in the Dal Lake, Cashmere, stands for the vacillating foundations of the Ecclesia, the catholic mother-church.

g) The Dal Lake near Srinagar and the prealps of the Himalaya in north-west India where Christ lived his second life and died at the incredible age of 114 years a natural demise

h) Titles: What occurred a f t e r Crucifixion ?

Christ survived the Cross in a miraculous way, with the help of God. Thus, the question after his further existence and deeds among humanity arises inevitably. The answer unveils a great surprise

The singular victory on the Cross

'The very moment Christ expired on the Cross, in a state of profound resignation, he started governing great parts of this world'

Part I: The book of doubts
This first part does accompany Christ from his birth up to the significative encounter with Saulus/Paulus at the gates of Damscus. Tradition leaves too many questions open, and the church does anwer too few

Part II: The book of (historical) truth
does reply, and resolve, a great many arbitrarily obscured facts of Christ's life

***

This small booklet represents a short introduction on the themes in the afore mentioned book of some 700 pages, entitled 'CHRIST-THE SCIENTIFIC PROOFS', in one publication consisting of two volumes, describing the great Nazarene's life under a historic-scientific aspect, from the well known primitive beginnings up to the drama on Calvary and the cru-cial encounter at Damascus. And furthermore the second, to us unknown life of Christ in the far away land of

India and at the natural end of the entirely extraordinary life, hidden to western Christianity for multiple reasons, of a personality destinated to become known to posteriority as the Son of God.

***

The trilogy, consisting of three volumes, entitled 'THE EPIC STORY OF CHRIST', based on proved historic facts, is a great epic and touching narrative situated in the antique roman, greek and judaean world. It starts with the uprise of the Maccabeean/Hasmonaean family of Galilee and its conquest of the royal title of Israel in 163 ante, accompanys every episode of the Nazarene's life up to Golgotha and Damascus and further on his travels to India and illustrates his activities and remarkable successes in the 'promised land' of Cashmere, his efforts in reforming Buddhism to a real world religion under the auspices of the king of Cashmere, and countless so far unknown events, right to his natural demise in Srinagar in the year 107 post - (after Christ!).

***

These books can be ordered at the folowing addresses:

Markus von Friedland   The author
Postfach No. 9852   Markus von Friedland
CH-8036 Zurich   Dr.h.c.
Switzerland

Fax: 0041 43 960 92 54
e-mail:
m_von_friedland@hotmail.com

BOD-Books on Demand Publications
Gutenbergring 53
D-22848-Norderstedt
Germany
Fax: 0049 (0)40 53 43 35 84

approximate costs: pages

	pages		
CHRIST: What happened...Introduction	60	Euro	20.-
CHRIST: Scientific proofs	700	Euro	49.-
CHRIST: The epic narrative-three volumes	1600	Euro	119.-

Christ

What happened after Golgotha?

(The enigmatic victory on the Cross)

Borne at Bethlehem
Crucified at Jerusalem   Burried in Cashmere, India

2. What it is about

Jesus Christ, the Epiphany of God on earth, is no doubt the most fascinating, but also the most enigmatic personality of the known world history. His appearance divided spirits and opinions already during his life time. In believers and those with sceptic attitude. He did impart on humanity a monstrous task: to live against the laws of nature, to protect the weak from the strong, to provide those by nature underprivileged with a bearable existence, to engage in battle against poverty - not against richness - and to abolish, and nothing less, wars and warlike conflicts with murder and assassination through milder forms of competition, without annihilation and torture of the enemy, by his great and suprising new command: 'Loveth (also) your Enemies!'

After roughly 2000 years of Christiandom, countless heavy errors have been committed, but a good part of the foregiven aim and (socio-political) program has, nevertheless, been achieved. Half the goal of the most spectacular command that had ever been ordered to history of men, has been accomplished. Not that the evil in this world had diminished, but the effects of evil on humanity as a whole has substantially decreased. It is thus not exaggerated to pretend that, inspite of largely existing and ever new miseries, around 2/3 of a tenfold larger humanity than at Christ's time do live to-day on this planet in better conditions than Adam and Eve in paradise.

*

3. Christ - Far more than the Messiah?

Actually, it ought to interest millions of people - and it truly does - to become to know more details on the dramatic circumstances of the life of this man amongst men and to be, eventually, in a position to distinguish poetry from truth through the mists of the past and to recognize the genuine, human person of Christ more clearly - and not the transfigured, ennobled and mystified aspect of the scriptures. We may anticipate the result: This urgently necessary correction may show us Christ in many ways unexpectedly different from the divine preacher in the gospels, but his undertakings appear even more fantastic and miraculous, and his divine gifts even more incomprehensible. And we are anew greatly impressed, exactly like the listeners of his time. His image and his reputation appear even more grandiose as we realize that the light he has come to kindle in this world started to shine as never before because of his incredible personal efforts, in conjunction with is exceptional talents - and that the part played in it by Godfather was very much scarcer than we did, so far, believe.

Already the birth of Jesus of Nazareth in an epoch of high political tensions between Rome and Jerusalem appears exceptional. Evidently, the great conjunction of the planets Jupiter and Saturn in the zodiac of Fishes in the year 7 ante a. (astronomic count) was interpretated as a precalculated heavenly sign for the birth of a prophezised Lord of the Universe, Duke of Peace or Lord of Salvation. The question be allowed if such a birth might have been part of a secret scheme of the so called religious section of the 'Silent in the Country', with the generation at the right time into the right family? In accordance, perhaps, with the foreseen appearance of the star of Bethlehem? Was it the birth of a 'prince-pretender' to the lost Hasmonaean throne who was expected, once grown up, to really dethronize king Herod's clan and with him to chase the Roman occupants out of Israel? Or could the arrival of the Magicians from the Orient, the later kings of Epiphany, indicate visitors from Persia and Northwest-India where Buddhism was practised and where, then about 500 years after the life of the historical Buddha, his re-incarnation was sought in Palestine, as foretold in Buddhist scriptures for about that time? Or would Christ simply be the expected Messiah, the anointed priestly king of Israel who would restore the old reign of king David in its ancient splen-dour? Or was he the purposly generated re-incarnation of the 'Master of Justice' who had founded, on the rims of the Dead Sea in the year 162 ante (historical modus) the famous mo-nastry of Qumran that became the predecessor of the Essenic Movement?

*

4. Jesus and John -
Secret heirs to the throne of an usurpated Dynasty?

There are numerous hints that the generation of Jesus, and also of his cousin John (the later Baptist), in one and the same family - was not fortuitous. Mary knew right from the beginning about an intimation and a promise about a son to be borne to her, then, at the tender age of only 15 years.

With certainty, Jesus spent the first part of his life with the thorough study of all available religious books and literature, but he grew up inmidst a numerous family with four known brothers and two sisters, all of them later children of his mother Mary. As the oldest son of the household he might have borne his part of the responsibility to nourish the family. An intense religious education in his early youth, about 8-12, a period of religious studies at the monastery of Qumran at the shores of the Dead Sea, are highly probable.

*

5. The erroneous interpretation of a Tibetan legend

A strange story about an extended voyage of young Jesus to India between his 13th and 28th year has recently received much publicity. But there are too many aspects contradicting and proving the story a fairy tale. The narration by Luke only on Jesus' presentation in the Herodian temple of Jerusalem at the age of 12 where he astonished the priests and religious authorities has, evidently, symbolical value only, as every jewish youth had to go through this procedure at the age of 12 to be admitted amongst grown up men. Or be it that Jesus had quite recently accomplished his early studies with the Essenic circles at Qumran and wanted now to demonstrate and prove his acquired religious knowledge of the scriptures in a discussion at the temple.

The tale about Jesus' wanderings with a commercial caravan to India which was discovered by the Russian traveller Nicolas Notovitch in the year 1887 in the Hemis-Monastery in Ladakh - we shall revert on this strange story in the course of this essay later - revealed itself after closer examination as a fake composition by later buddhist chroniclers. But - such chronics would never have been written abvout Jesus in the far lands of India and Tibet had he not appeared there really, but much later, - after his Resurrection in Jerusalem, and had he not personally related the events in his motherland Palestine and over his own crucifixion.

Both youths, Jesus and John, were actually borne as secret heirs to the Hasmonaean dynasty (also called the Maccabees) who had lost their throne and power in the year 34 ante to the Romans who, on their turn, set Herod on their throne. But they grew up in a time where political re-conquest of Palestine from the Romans was absolutely out of question. Thus, they started, once grown up, on the truly fantastic vision of installing a Celestial Kingdom on earth, with the assent of God, and acting as his herolds. John was six months older than Jesus, and it was thus up to him to start the first attempt. Being age-wise second to him in the bid for the throne, Jesus submits to John in occasion of the baptism at the Jordan river. For the time being. - For a long time Jesus had waited for John's challenge. But when John fell victim through decapitation on the Herod Antipas' fortress of Machairus in Transjordania as a result of the intrigues of Salome and Herodias against the king, things took a radical change. Jesus withdraws for ten months to the north, to Galilee, and we hear nothing from him. It's a time of absolute silence and inner preparation.

*

6. The great, long Silence

Jesus and John the Baptist had, apparently, quite contro-
versial opinions on the mission amongst the Samaritan people, living in the area north of Judaea and Jerusalem. Until
that time, Jesus had preached the word of God in the sense of
John's message to the people of Israel, and there was no visible enmity against him. Also the celebrated scene of the cleaning of the holy temple with the whip amongst the money
changers occured in this period and was tolerated as a zelotic
act of invocation for Judaea to do penance and prepare for the
incumbing end of the world. But now, after parting from John
and his circle, Jesus remains silent for almost ten months in
the north, in Galilee, and prepares his own come-back. Suddenly, he re-appears, but this time with a revolutionary teaching. In that spring of 31 post h (historic count), he breaks
away from the holy Thora, but also from Qumran out of which
movement at the shores of the Dead Sea, both he and John,
had once emerged. Jesus engages himself with contradicting
quite a series of over-sophisticated and unrealistic religious
laws that determined the daily ways of antique Judaism (....but
I tell you that..). He vehemently opposes the petrified religious
formalism of his days and conjures a new bountiful Fathergod
of Compassion from the skies. It is none but him who dares to
transform the angry and often revengeful God of Old Israel
and Moises into a God of kindness, indulgence and fore-
giveness. Nobody before him would ever have dared to
address the ineffable name of Jahwe by the simple term of
'Father in the Heavens'. This alone was, then and still now, an
unsupportable blasphemy in the ears of believing Jews.

The disciples of Christ were the choice of the first hour. But
pretty soon it became evident that none of them could
possibly match the high pretensions to reach the goal Jesus
was aiming at. In the dramatic plan that was ripening on
Jesus' mind, they could at best play an inferior role. The main
actors had to be of a different cut. People of rank and influence would have to take the lead to bring Christ's super-
human project to success, if God would support it. - Jesus
struggled desperately for his own identiy. Whom do you say I
am? he asked his disciples with questioning tone in his voice,

as reported in the gospels. Jesus of Nazareth, borne into an impoverished royal and priestly family, fatherless, with Hasmonaean ancesters on his mother's side and adoptive descent from the house of king David on his stepfather Joseph's side, entrusted with secret promises over his Messiahship, cherished by nature with a flawless and stately appearance, at least one head taller than most of his jewish countrymen, gifted with formidable intelligence and miraculous healing powers, would not know for a very long time what role he was destined to play and what God's intention for him was.

For long years he used to pray to his heavenly Father to reveal him his own identity. But while we constantly read from the prophets of Old Israel that God had spoken to them in order that they should profess God's will to his people, we never hear anything similar about Christ. He prays day and night to his Father, but we never hear about the words of the Father to him. Eventually, Jesus comes to the conclusion that he cannot possibly be the prophezised political Messiah, nor the prince-pretender to the royal priestly throne, nor the simple rebirth of the 'Teacher of Rightousness' who had founded the order of the Essenes at Qumran. Slowly but inevitably it dawns on his mind with secret consternation: I am the Son of Man out of the books by Henoch, I am the Son of God, an avatar of the Highest on earth amongst men. And he realizes quickly and fully the extreme dangerousness of such a role. This explains his extreme prudence of expression and all thinkable measures taken to conceal his real identity, even amongst his disciples and his entourage of women. He has decided to accept his role and to speak up for his Fathergod and to bring down and inaugurate the Celestial Kingdom on earth, in the name of God. But he himself has to remain incognito, if he was to succeed in his glorious undertaking.

But the people would not listen to him. The success of his tremendous endevours is rather trifling. His compatriots take willingly advantage of his extraordinary healing capacities, they are impressed by his teachings about a new mankind, new morals and the new character of God, but one does not understand or is not ready to accept his allusions and concealed interpretations of his self. The consequences are too monstrous: What to think about an apparently human being who says: 'Where I am the Celestial Kingdom is right in your midst', and: 'I am the Path, the Light and the Life', although he has flesh and blood? - Such like people around him may have thought, and his disciples may often have felt in similar ways.

*

7. Was an alteration of consciousness in the game?

Jesus demonstrates an outspoken sense for dramatical effects. He seems to be perfectly aware that he can only succeed by compelling God to accredit and confirm him as his son and representative in public on the holiest day of the year, the Passah, at the holiest location of the country of the Jews, in front of the Great Temple. Should God, however, keep silent and not intervene at all, then Jesus would have become victim of a terrible misvalutation of himself. Then he would have fully deserved to be executed as a false and perilous prophet and preacher: Out of resignation in face of incumbant defeat it is that Jesus' world-moving masterplan of the drama on Golgotha takes shape.

We shall never be able to fully understand the conditions of Jesus' self-consciousness, which is unique in this world. Neither shall we know whether or not Jesus suffered from any form of paranoia which may have induced him into the megalomania to believe to be God himself, or whether there where drugs or poisons at work that may have altered his state of consciousness. Many a hint there is, amongst else the gnostic ascensions to heaven, the dreamlike elevation up to God which, according to the 'Secret Gospel' he ought to have celebrated with his closest disciples only, during long nightly rites, not unlike the greek mystery festivities which used to take place in greatest secrecy. It is evident that he decided to challenge Godfather himself on the Cross, in all humility, and that he knitted a network of connections to high ranking people belonging to the 'Silent in the Country', during the winter 31/32 post h, while he was alone in Jerusalem, to people who would be able and willing to assist him in his incredible task. But it is also irrefutable that Jesus, when asked by the president of the Jewish Synhedrium of 72 gathered councellors and religious tribunal in the decisive moment on the early morning of Good Friday replied on the crucial question: 'Are you it?' (meaning the Messiah), clearly: 'ANI HU' (meaning: I am HIM). This did not simply mean: Yes, I am. Jesus used in his reply the holiest theophanic formula in Jewish liturgy, meaning, above any possible doubts: 'Yes, I am HIM (God in person!) who speaks to you'. Only such an unexpected theophanic reply could lead to the immediate death sentence by the vote of an evidently vast majority of the councel, and to the practical execution.

In the light of thorough historical investigation, it would clearly appear that every step of the drama of Golgotha was precisely pre-planned, be it the Cenaculum, the betrayal by Judas in Gethsemane, the arrestation, the trial before the Roman procurator Pontius Pilate, and eventually the cruxi-fiction itself. And equally all measures taken for a possible salvation and rescue from the Cross. But it is also clear that neither the disciples, nor the women did have the slightest idea of what was really happening.

*

8. ...And w h o m do you say I a m ?

The danger that the plan may be betrayed if the disciples were initiated into it was far too great. Thus, everybody's task might correspond to a little wheel in the ambitous scenario that would go into action on Passah. But nobody could realize the impact of this plan except for Jesus alone. Since he could not possibly foretell the judgement of God, he had to act in a way to keep all possibilities of his role open in case of salvation, also that of being confirmed as the Messiah, or as the Son of God, or the Son of Man in the sense of the (prophet)-Henoch tradition of the Old Testament, or as the king of Jews out of the royal hoiuse of Hasmon and as the predicted Messiah in a culminative office. Or as none of them all. The prophets had promised in the scriptures that the coming Messiah would triumphantly enter Jerusalem on the back of a she-ass, that he would erect the Realm of God on earth in occasion of Passah, and that he would announce and open the happy period of the end of all times. Jesaia speaks in his great prophesies of the upright Just who would appear at that stage, of the suffering servant of God who would be whipped, tortured, and flagellated, but who's bones would not be broken and who - after having done penitence and have suffered on behalf of his people, should eventually be miraculously saved by God.

Every imaginable preparation was made in order to comply with these prophesies and to create the necessary suppositions for the descent of God and his Celestial Kingdom on earth on that Passah 32 post h (historic count). Quite obviously, Jesus was firmly convinced that, first of all, th prophecised conditions had to be arranged for, in order to induce God to redeem and honour His once given promises. Jesus of Nazareth had wanted to be tried, accused and executed at the hour and the place determined by him, and alone by him, and at he same time he had taken all possible preparative action and dispositions to make it possible for God to grant his survival - if He then wanted to. Christ himself trembled in face of the enormity of his project to encounter at the hour chosen by him and on his own initiative the Allmighty and sweated in the garden of Gethsemany tears of fear, once for the hideous tortures he was to expect, but also - that his capture might not take place at all, or too late.

'Father, let this bitter cup pass me - but They will occur, not mine' he prayed fervently. Jesus is not ready to die; he wants to propagate his new sight of the world and his new teaching further amongst men, with the assistance and help of the Father in the heavens. Yet, the task is too gigantic, he feels unable to accomplish it ever without the active intervention of God Himself. He is full of hope that God might thus save him out of the claws of his enemies and present him, in front of the entire multitude and the whole people as his only an Oneborne Son, or as the promised Messiah, or as his ambassador amongst men, or He might accept his sacrifice and reject him if he, Jesus, should have profoundly erred. Rather confusing and striking is the fact that the great prophets of Israel lead at all times direct dialogues and consequently spread the results, advices and admonitions of God with prominent voices among the people of Israel. Not so Jesus. He transmits the word of God in his own name...: I, however, say on to you... . Never did he designate himself as prophet and thus as mediating voice of God. Because he is more than a prophet, more than the Messiah, more than the Son of Man; he is an an Epiphany of God Himself on earth. - But only he knows it: 'Nobody knoweth the Father but he to whom the son shall manifest him'. And: 'All has been given over to me by the Father, in the heavens and on earth'. He will have to reveal now soon the great secret of his identity, which was known to the disciples only very vaguely and which had never been reconfirmed by the master before. Then, however, immediate execution will be inevitable. The mode of execution that stood on blasphemy was crucifixion. And the question was: How could possible survival be obtained, and death be prevented in spite of actual crucifixion inflicted by an impartial Roman jurisdiction and a highly and technically perfected application of the death sentence?

Jesus arranges for the Sedermeal one day before the national usance (which would have been on friday, the day of actual crucifixion), in compliance with the Essenic ritual in which, contrary to the official Thora prescriptions, men only took part, within the city walls in great secret, in the house of a priest's son, John, his beloved disciple. He does take really leave since he himself does not count on salvation as he received, evidently, no assertion from above on his prayers. And if a miracle occurred and he should be saved, then surely not in an earthly body. Entirely in a gnostic sense he introduces a mystical ritual for the sigillation and conjuration of the New Alliance and the new interpretation of the Allmighty as a God of Compassion. His blood and his flesh sould become an eternal sign for the forces of Light against those of Darkness. And the compassion of God over all creature.

Judas has been charged to communicate the exact place of Jesus' presence that night of the 'betrayal', to the Jewish authorities. But Judas does not know why he must do this. He does it, simply because ordered to him by the master. Eventually, it is Jesus himself who tells him precisely when he should go. Now. Not earlier, and not later. When Judas begins to realize to what his 'betrayal' has actually led, he commits suicide by hanging himself on a tree. Or has he been murdered to avoid that his part in that plan became known and would endanger the success of the whole grandiose undertaking?

9. The theophanic formula: ANI HU - Yes, I am HIM!

The capture takes place in the night at the shine of torches. Then there follows, at sundawn, in quick sequence the trials. First before the old highpriest Hannas, then before the hastily convocated Synhedrium, the accusation, the contradicting wittnesses, the crucial question by the acting high priest Joseph Kaiphas: 'Are YOU it?' -Until now, Jesus kept silent. According to the texts by Jesaia, the Suffering Just of God does not defend himself. Jesus could continue to be taciturn. Or he could give hundredfold uncompromising replies. He does not. It is the 'Hora Revelationis', the hour of revelation of the great truth: 'ANI HU! we hear him say. Clearly and distinctly. The Great Council keep their breath. Consternation, followed by unanimous rage. Kaiphas tears his cloth apart. The counsellors imitate him, one after the other. The inexpressible has been uttered: 'I am HIM (God who stands before you)'. This is the most holy theophanic formula which JAHWE alone is entitled to be addressed with.

Jesus of Nazareth did, with full consciousness, provoke his immediate death-sentence. The proofs would not have been sufficient. The trial had been led impeccably according to the valid laws. Now, the sentenced culprit is conducted to the Roman procurator, Pontius Pilate, who alone can confirm, or not, the deadly sentence, since not too long ago, the Romans had prohibited the enactment of blood sentences to the Jewish government. Pilate does not see the point, he presumes a trap of the always sly Jewish politicians, to get him caught. He tries to get rid of the case and asks: 'Galileean he is? - Then, I am not competent. Bring him to the king over his own province, Herod-Antipas', who had also come for the Passah festivities to Jerusalem.

But also the murderer of John the Baptist, king Herod-Antipas, is not able to get a single word out of the prisoner in front of him. Disappointed not to see a miracle done by Jesus, he commands to have his 'guest' hung a royal purple coat over the shoulders, in mockery, and sends him back to Pilate.

Great haste is now important. The clock advances fastly towards noon.

10. The Master's plan

The crucifixion has to take place in the early friday-afternoon, in order to shorten the duration of the torture on the Cross and preserve the chances of survival. If crucifixion started too early, hanging on the patibulum might last dangerously long, but if the execution should be too much delayed, it might be postponed until after Passah as executions on a Sabbath and on Passah, wich in that occasion fell exceptionally together, are prohibited by religious jewish law. In that case, any chances of (natural) survival would be annihilated and death would be inevitable. This, exactly, has to be avoided. This aspect, and foresight, might also partially explain the ob-stinate silence of Jesus at court. Had he tried to defend himself and provoke a discussion, most valuable time would have been lost. But in this way, the whole procedure takes its premeditated course. The crucifixion can take place shortly before noon (at about the 6th hour, or 12 noon). The religious Sabbath rules prescribe that no person may be hanging on crosses over the most holy weekend that stood before. After sunset, also touching a corpse was forbidden with orthodox, thus believing Jews. It was thus foreseeable that the persons tried and tortured on the crosses would have to be taken down before Sabbath began, that means by sunset. And thus it happened. Everything could be anticipated. Given these circumstances, three aspects had been considered and respective solutions pondered upon: Jesus had to be brought to complete unconsciousness and totally lifeless appearance, and this swiftly. Next, the breaking of his leg bones which was customary on such occasions to quicken death of the victims by suffocation had to be avoided by all means. And ultimately, the unsuspected rescue of the apparent death body by secret friends and followers into a secure hiding place had to be operated.

This, thus, is what exactly happened. Precise agreements had been taken with influental and reliable personalities out of the circle of the 'Silent in the Country', those secret followers of the new teachings of Jesus who expected, together with him, the coming down of the Celestial Realm through Godfather and who believed in Christ's mission. Most certainly, there must have been quite a number of such persons involved, but only two of them are shortly introduced by their names in the evangelic gospels. Interestingly enough a medical doctor, named Nicodemus, a jew with a hellenistic name and member of the supreme Council, the same as Joseph of Arimathaea who was equally a member of the great Synhedrium, highest religious and political jewish authority at Jerusalem. They were thus members of the same supreme Council that had, in the late forenoon, sentenced Christ to death by an over-whelming majority of votes. Another memnber of the Council and reputed teacher of the Thora of the pharisaeic section who also secretly supported the cause of Jesus, might have been the Gamaliel I, well known by historians. Strange enough, shortly after Jesus 'had given up the spirit' as the di-sciple John reports in his gospel as an eyewitness and while while his body hung apparently lifeless on the Cross, Nicodemus entered the scene on Golgotha, evidently to judge the state of health conditions, and to prevent the Roman execution team from inflicting deadly blows on the apparent corpse of Christ. This occured while Joseph of Arimathaea hurried over to the fortress Antonia, near the Great Temple, to obtain from the Roman procurator the allowance to take Jesus' body down from the cursed gallow-Cross and to give it a descent burrial. - This, then, was the most critical phase of the plan.

*

11. Did poison foster apparent death on the Cross?

When Jesus, hanging on the Cross, said after completion of his prayer: 'I am thirsty', a sponge was stuck on an Ysop rod, pretendingly soaked with vinagdre and gall. Such a mixture would usually stir the blood circulation and smoothen the pain. To the surprise of many, the result of this assistance was a sudden collapse. Was there anything more in that sponge? Possibly a poison, won out of the so called 'Schwalbenwurz' (swallow-root), out of which also the myste-rious Soma-beverage of the ancient Vedas in the steps of Central Asia and in India was brewed for their religious rituals? This very plant is still called 'Judaswurz' in the land of Tyrol (root of Judas). Trance, profound unconsciousness and temporary disorder of eyesight could be the consequence. This some-brewage was possibly also a part in the nightly mistery celebrations which are cited in the so called 'Secret Gospel', and it cannot be excluded that any such beverage might have been the cause of the trance and temporary blindness of Saulus/Saint Paul, in occasion of his encounter with Christ outside of Damascus.

One could also guess the employment of another highly poisenous plant of the Solaneazaea botanical family, the so called 'Sodom apple'. The yellow, spheric little fruits of this plant ripen - as the case may be - exactly in march and april at the edge of the Dead Seain Palestine, where in ancient times the biblic cities of Sodom and Gomorrah stood - and spring was also the time of crucifixion. Up to this day, the poison of these fruits is in Arabia (Yemen) well known for causing catalepsy and apparent death if consumed in sufficient quantity. Is it thinkable that, in occasion of the death of Lazarus, related only in the gospel of John, who died only some 2-3 weeks before the events on Golgotha, the summministration of the necessary dose of the poison was tested - to last at least some 30 hours?

On the Cross, Jesus prayed the 22nd pslam of the patriarchs, in accordance with tradition the longer part with murmering voice, thus hardly intelligible to listeners at his feet, decisive parts howerver with raised voice, loudly and clearly, in partdicular the end of this psalm which goes: ..it is ACCOMPLISHED! -Immediately after sipping out of the soaked sponge on the rod, Jesus cried out: 'My God, my God, why hathst thy forsaken me? -This is a scandalon in christian tradition ever which nobody would have dared to simply invent. The christian churches had their headaches with this cry of disperation of the Son of God from the Cross, all the way down through 20 centuries. No doubt, the tradition tells the truth. And no matter in what way it was tried to embellish or distort the meaning of this historical shout of desperation, its significance remains unchangeably the same: Total dispair of Christ in the very last seconds before unconsciousness overcomes him on the Cross. Godfather has abandoned, apparently, his counterfeit on earth in the fleshly person of Jesus. He did nothing to save his valiant believer. Jesus' self-interpretation was, seemingly, totally wrong, and the death-sentence on him as religious seducer of his people appeared justified. Its the ultimate defeat. Allthough he knows about all the arranged preparations for his bodily salvation in case Godfather should fail to intervene, the situation appears hopeless to the point that dying Jesus tends to capitulate and not to believe anymore in a divine miracle. - On which he might have had his sincere doubts right from the beginning of his Passion.

While Joseph of Arimathaea spoke to the governor, Pilate, at his palace and while the latter sent a centurion to Golgotha to ascertain that the crucified Jesus had already died - the footway from the rock of the skull, Calvary, to the Roman headquarters, the fortress Antonia, may have been some 15 minutes walk - the other member of Israel's supreme Council, Nicodemus, tried to convince the Roman officer in charge of executions, Longinus by name, that the victim of Nazareth had really already died. His efforts found open ears, more so as he could prove to be a doctor of medicine and as he does not appear to be known to anybody on the scene as a secret disciple of Christ. Nevertheless, even if a certain sympathy for the accused transgressor was shown, he was bound to make sure beyond doubts that death had occurred; otherwise, his own life would be at stake. In th presence of the Roman centurion, the officer Longinus pushes his long, slender, sharp-pointed lance up into Jesus' body - but not on the side of the heart - between the rips six and seven. The result is a cut of about 10 cm in width, out of which spurges blood and water immediately, as testified by thast disciple and eye-witness of the crucifixtion, John, in his gospel. John was by that time in his twenties only, and a cute observer. Evidently, the Roman officer had hit a pouch under the skin filled with water, without however penetrating deep into the body. No vital organ was hurt. But Jesus showed nevertheless not the least reaction anymore and hung, apparently lifeless, on the Cross. Conseguently, the permission for the unusally early deposition of the body from the Cross was given by the Roman procurator, Pilate. Even he could not, at this critical point of his career, allow himself any serious political error, in spite of his blood-hound reputation. This because his mentor and protector, Sejanus who had governed the Roman Empire instead of the exiled emperor Tiberius on Capri, had been arrested, accused of political betrayal, conspiration and usurpation against the emperor and had lost his life in Rome through decapitation. These circumstances explain the unexpectedly mild and considerate behavour of Pilate towards Christ during his trial. This was later interpretated, in christian circles, erroneously as a pro-christian attitude - which it certainly was not, even if Pilate's respect shown to the person of the accused Nazarene might have been genuine.

*

12. Christ - Burried alive

Jesus may have been taken down from the Cross in the 11th hour, towards 17.00 h our time. As we know from the evangelists, only a few hundred yards away a sepulchre cut out of the rock was ready in the private garden of Joseph of Arimathaea. This peculiar circumstance alone is worthy of attention: a provisional sepulchre on private grounds, i.e. not accessible to the public and thus a sort of a hiding place, forbidden for the women, the disciples and other followers - or enemies -, just on the edge of the rock of Golgotha, a public execution place, obviously foreseen as such also for Jesus? There they brought the body of Christ. Tradition tells that the women of the suit of Jesus brought about 50 pounds (!) of ointments and aloe, and a very costly funeral linen.

All that could could not possibly have been bought on that precarious Good Friday afternoon of the crucifixion, on the day before the saintly jewish Sabbath - but days before. Jesus was not treated as dead as soon as his body was brought to comparative security, out of reach of Roman soldiers and the public, but like a heavely wounded person. His body was carefully covered with antiseptic wound ointments, with myrrh concentrates that are being used up to our time against blood poisoning and infections. His body was stiffly and warmly wrapped up and his head was deposited on a sort of stone cushion to prevent suffocation through hemorrhagy out of the lungs. On his face, a camphor-drenched cloth was pressed, to enhance respiration. Then, the sepulchre was closed by rolling a huge round cut millingstone like a lock of stone into tracks in front of the entrance. And it cannot be excluded that one or two assistants from the order of the Essenes, dressed entirely in white - appearing later in the gospels as angel-like youths - shut themselves with the body of Christ in the tomb for medical care and surveillance and pushed the rollstone gate open from the inside on early sunday morning before dawn, when Christ had re-awakend to consciousness. And thus put to flight with this horror-scene a possible grave-watch, consisting of unexperienced volunteers hired by the Temple authorities, and on no account by Roman soldiers or regular Temple guards - if any kind of a watch there really was.

It is a fact that the sepulcral linen, now conserved in the dome of Turin, Italy, has been scientifically examined in the mean-time, not only by scientists in the service of the Vatican, but independantly also by several temas of experts of the NASA, Houston, USA, and that all investigations have come to the conclusion that the linen is unquestionably genuine. In 1988 the Vatican had declared the Turin linen as a medieval fraud as a result of an equally fraudulent carbon-14 test, but in 1991 the Catholic church revised their sentence which saw in this linen a fake, and recognized officially the authenticity of the linen as the one of Christ. It is in fact the original tunica in which the body of Christ, deposed from the Cross, was wrapped. This cloth was drenched with the blood of Christ which was shed after deposition, in the long hours in the sepulchre, by his body. Thus, there is a proof of a weak heart activity, as a corpse does not shed life-blood anymore; coa-gulated death blood has a quite different consistency and no halos of serum around the blood stains as are still visibles in the linen.

Interesting to note also that orthodox Jews, such as Christ's disciples where, were not allowed to touch a dead body on the imminence of the holy Sabbath that had already begun - what they would have done, if the body were a corpse. The urgent medical treatment by his followers took undoubtedly place after sunset on that friday, in the beginning darkness, for pro-tection from unauthorized eyes.

*

13. Challenge on the Patibulum of Condemnation

No doubt, Christ hads survived his crucifixion in a marculous and unexpected way with the help of God - or of his own? Precisely as the prophets had foretold. And as he had desired it so intensely himself. He had been saved by God and brought back into his old life, although with a gesture of admonition by the Father for the son's extravagant method of challenge on the Cross.

Jesus of Nazareth had promised the imminent descent of the Celestial Kingdom of God on earth, but the years were passing, and nothing happened. The Roman military force in the country was stronger than ever before. And the pression of expectations with regard to the promised arrival, or revelation, of the Messiah grew daily. Jesus saw himself more and more compelled towards action and decision taking if he did not want to risk to loose the dynamic of enthusiasm and firm believe of his disciples and his adherents. Ever more now, a dramatic culmination of events took shape and appeared inevitable and necessary.

Christ eventually went on the Cross for an apocalyptical battle, which he, apparently, lost. But in reality he won it, thanks to the genius of his preparations, the self-betrayal by Judas in Gethsemany, the most able obtainment of a quick death sentence as a consequence of his use of the most sacred theophanic formula of Israel, the choice of the exact hour for his own crucifixion, the summiministration of the tossico-narcotic brewage in the sponge at the Cross at the right moment, the almost immediate deposition from the Cross, the rapid evacuation of his motionless body by friendly hands to the hiding place in Joseph of Arimathaea's new cut tomb and the intensive healing treatments of his wounds in the grave.

His prayers in Gethsemany had been heard in heaven. But he had escaped real death very narrowly and with much luck. Many a thing could have taken a quite unhappier turn. Particularly critical moments were Pilate's initial refusal to confirm the death sentence to the Jewish authorities, then the not foreseeable idea of Pilate to have his prisoner sent over to the tetrarch of Galilee, king Herodes Antipas who was also present in Jerusalem, on hearing that Jesus was a Galileean. Eventually, the amnesty of Barrabas instead of his, the sudden fall in the via Dolorosa crashing on the ground with arms tied up at the patibulum and breaking his nose bone which certainly was an additional tremendous handicap for breathing on the Cross. Furthermore, the certainly not plan-ned lance-stroke in his (wrong!) side and the scepticism of Pilate about Jesus' so early demise. And blood-poisoning and other deadly complications could easily have occurred.

Christ had considered all these risks and, quite obviously, given very little chance to his own survival. This assumption is confirmed by his attitude: Final wellfare from his disciples, institution of the Cenacular Rite of the New Alliance, to be repeated in his memory, the confiding of his own mother Mary to the young disciple John from the Cross, the shout of despair from the Cross: 'Father, my Father, why hathst thou forsaken me!?'-On this day of Sabbath, there was yet no question of anything like a resurrection on the overnext day. Such a feature had also never been prophezised anywhere. The mourning of the disciples and the women is genuine - they had never been initiated in the great secrecy of the Master's plan.

But resurrection was accomplished. With the energetic and secret help of friends out of the circle of the 'Silent in the country' (Saints) who also expected the descent of the Celestial Kingdom, together with novizes and laizistic sympathizers of the Essenic order of the Dead Sea. These went about clad in a white robe, like Jesus himself, in an unsewed frock-coat. Probably, they belonged to the Galileean sect of the Nazorenes (from 'nezer' = sprout). These assistants helped Jesus out of the tomb shortly before dawn on that early Easter-morning. In fact, Mary Magdalena appears as the first visitor at the tomb even before sundawn - and misses by minutes to become an eyewitness of the resurrection. The white-clad youths are still sitting in the tomb chamber (described as 'angels') and did not have the time to evacuate the place and avoid Mary Magdalena. Jesus had been led away shortly before, had tried his first steps in that cemetary-garden when he too was surprised by the unexpected early arrival of Mary. In the oldest gospel, by Mark, there is no mention at all of a grave-watch at that time. Jesus' body is covered with wounds, but non of them proved fatal. He is literally envelopped into a large and long coat with a cowl over his head, as he has to leave the place with all his hurting wounds without being recognized.

One of the youths who sat in the sepulchre (!) said those famous words to Mary: 'Why searchethst thou among the dead him who dwells amongst the living? - He is not here, but resurrected'! (Quid quaeretis viventem cum mortuis - non est hic, sed surrexit!). - Not even Mary recognizes him, until Jesus calls her: 'Mary!' But now she recognizes his voice and answers back: 'Rabbuni!', sinking to his feet and trying to embrace his legs. But he rejects her: 'Don't touch me! - I have not yet ascended to my Father.' After 42 strokes of flagellation his body is aching everywhere and any contact is extremely painful. This circumstance is immediately understandable. But what does the enigmatic explanation mean? - At this instance, also Jesus is taken by surprise to find himself again amongst the living. He does hardly realize whether or not he is really still alive, and if so: why? Does he yet expect the trans-figuration of his body to enable him to ascend to his Father in heaven? All signs indicate that Mary, in love with her Master, knew since his deposition from the Cross that there was still hope of survival of Jesus and that, therefore, she appeared too early at the tomb and was full of consternation to find the grave empty because she had had a presentment that this tomb did not really shelter a corpse. Jesus had, evidently, not expected to survive after all his sufferings, in particular not after realizing on the Cross that God would not visibly intervene to save and take him from the Cross. At that very moment he cannot yet grasp what had happened, what it all meant and what the will of God would really be.

The fact that Jesus had survived the Cross is nowadays widely accepted in scientific circles initiated to the theme, including the hundreds of specialists that have worked on a string of examinations and analysis of the Holy Shround, and including the leading authorities of the Vatican. A part of the above exposed logic arguments and conclusions, there is the

Holy Shroud of Turin in which Christ's body was bedded after deposition from the Cross. This Shroud does show numerous blood stains, around which circles of blood-serum can still be proved. Even the American Space Authorities, NASA, had led intensified studies on those rustlike stains on the Shroud and came, after two years of debate, pro and contra, to the irrevocable result: Those stains are human blood. No colour, no chemicals, no oxydes, no fakes of a painter. Blood!. The blood of Christ, because the Shroud shows exactly those injuries mentioned by tradition in the original gospels: The injury caused by the crown of thorns, the lance-slide on the right (!) side of the thorax, the 2 x 21 strokes of flagellation on back and legs, the greatly swollen right cheek, the broken nose bone from the crash on the floor of Via Dolorosa, the heavy scorches over the left shoulder caused by friction of the roughly cut wooden patibulum. All this is visible and provable. Furthermore, the entire body-print in the linen of a 1,83 m tall man. With a physically perfectly grown body. With facial traits one does not easily forget, orderly combed and parted red-blond hear and beard hair, with mild yet authoritative and dignified expression of the face, obviously capable of both tears and wrath, with a secret charisma of intelligence and compassion.

*

14. The Holy Shroud of Turin (The Linen)

A face that never laughed, a mouth that professed words of boundless compassion, but that could also leas speeches of mighty wrath (according to a report by the Syrian Legate Lentulus, appointed by the Romans). The blood stains in the Shroud do prove that the heart activity had never entirely ceased in the tomb, as dead persons do not bleed anymore. But it does also prove that Jesus did not die as a consequence of the tortures on the Cross, since we do encounter him still afterwards on several occasions. Until Damascus, 1 1/2 years after crucifixion. The question thus arises in a compelling way: If he had not died, neither been taken up into the skies, and accepting once the standpoint of the Nestorians, the Chaldeans, the Armeniens and the church of Syria who all knew that Crist had survived, where and when, then, did he really die, and what did he possibly accomplish during his second, recovered life?

The Holy Shroud of Turin had been declared, in the year 1988, by the Vatican as a medieval fake after having been determined by chemical examinations (C-14 radio carbon tests) on miniscule pieces of the linen in Arizona, England and Zurich that resulted out of threads woven into the Shroud in the 14th century in France. The outcome of such chemical analysis could, of course, please the Vatican - who could have got rid of a most intriguing question and problem regarding the entire Christiandom. But most unfortunately for the church, not the Shroud did prove a fake, but the cloth-threads delivered to the three laboratories for examination. Such analysis had, anyway, been requested for exclusively from the protestant side and had taken place accordingly in exclusively protestant surroundings. It was afterwards discovered that the three cloth examples put at the three universities disposal for the C-14 radio carbon tests - had been taken out of the rim of the Holy Shround of Turin and thus areas that had been mended in the middle ages by nuns by the end of the 13th century, because the bords of the linen had greatly suffered from the continous touchings of the believers when exposed for catholic festivities in France.

It would all appear that the dispatch of those wrong cloth-threads of linen did not happen inarbitrarily... In any case, the mother church in Rome did have the courage to withdraw its negative verdict of the year 1988 in february 1991 and accept officially that the Holy Shroud of Turin is the original grave-linen of Jesus Christ. But only after vehement protests and inherent publications of a series of scientists and professors who did accuse the catholic church of monstrous fraud. The Holy Shroud of Christ continues thus to be conserved and safeguarded in the chapel of the dome of Turin, after Pope John Paul II had on purpose flown to Lisbon in 1983 to obtain this most important relique of Christianity from the then dying last Italian king Umberto II, out of the house of Savoy, who had been that far the legal propriator of the linen.

And why blood, and no chemicals or colour-oxydes??

One experiment that was conducted directly on the Shroud was the so-called x-ray 'fluorescent-spectral analysis' with the help of which it became eventually possible to prove with certainty that the supposed blood stains were r e a l l y blood. A section of the linen would be exposed, for a very short time, to a high dosis of x-rays which made the cloth itself beaming - it became fluorescent. Since every kind of molecule does become fluorescent in its own particular way under influence of high energies, it is possible to ascertain the atomic structure of the x-rayed material comparing it with a spectrum of fluoroscopy. These stains on the Shroud show particularly high quantities of the iron element. Iron, however, is one of the main substances of blood.

The overquick assumption by the American chemical scientist Dr.W.Crowne that this circumstance could signify colour with high iron contents which, however, came into use first in the 15th century only, and not earlier, would quickly be counter-proved by treating parts of the linen with vapours of hydrazine and formic acid and exposing it thereafter to ultraviolet light beams. In this test, molecules of porphyrine shine up in red. Porphyrine occurs in a stadium of hemo-building up and is accepted as infallible proof for the presence of blood, even though the hem itself had been destroyed by the influence of great heat.

Once the experts of NASA could have proved that the fallow redish stains on the linen were, unquestionably, human blood of the rare blood group AB, the problem of an at first supposed fake cloth out of the middle ages was, basically, resolved. Since it is unthinkable that any human painter or artist should have painted a naked man, front and back side, two bodies in one line, the two heads almost touching in the middle, and the whole picture inverted, like a photo negative using for the marking of injuries genuine human blood - living blood!

The question to be asked now could only be: In what century there lay a naked, tortured man in this cloth who had exactly the injuries reported for Christ by the gospel writers? For this purpose the real age of the tissue had to be determined with accuracy.

The earlier analysis in the centre of the Holy Shroud had already clearly pointed to the age of the New Testament of the bible. On the one side, the linen had been woven in a so called fish-spine pattern which was typical for Syria in biblical times. Such technics of weaving were entirely unknown in the Europe of the middle ages. Furthermore, a considerable amount of plant polls had been discovered in the cloth from plants that still do exist in Palestine, Syria and Turkey only, which virtually confirms the historically known travel route of the Shroud.

The reliable dating of the linen through the C-14 radio carbon test was yet not possible until the year 1987 because too large pieces of tissue would have had to be sacrificed . Eventually, a method of the C-14 carbon test was developped for which only a few threads would be needed. But: The examined threads originated out of mended patches at the rim of the Shrould - which made the results of the tests a farce.

This leads us to the next question of importance: How did this extremely strange kind of negative printlike image of a whole body and face, front and back side, actually occur on this cloth?

Some sindologists (scientific researchers of the Shroud) condivided the opinion that this picture-print on the tissue could have occurred through a kind of supranatural rays of heat to which Jesus' body might have been exposed at the very moment of the resurrection and that by that release of high energy the body picutre was 'burnt' into the linen. But since the outlines of the body are not at all fluorescent on x-rays application, the creation by heat involvement from outside must be discarded entirely. In addition, any sort of heat energy rays would have penetrated the thin linen completely, whereas the body picture visible on the cloth is due to an alteration of the textile fibre tips at the surface only.

But how did the picture then evolve?

As replies to this question there had been developed a remarkable series of fantastic hypothesis, ever since the discovery of this extraordinary photo negative/positive phenomena by the Italian photographer Secondo Pia in the year 1898, and which all belong, one more one less, into the realm of fantasy.

In the meantime, a series of trials have shown that there are also quite simple and natural ways to obtain a reproduction that is similar to the one on the Turin Shroud.

The results of such experiments by American exports show that the sepia-coloured darker patches in the picture on the Shroud have been caused by alteration of the chemical structure of the cellulose of the linen. Labor tests obtained similar colour shade differenciations as on the cloth by destroying the cellulose of linen under influence of various products of oxydation. Such oxydation-pictures tend to become even sharper outlines by ageing.

As early as 1924 the French biology professor, Paul Vignon, did have considerable success with his experiments of the so called 'theory of vapourographism'. Vignon proved already by then that a sweating body, put into a linen that had been previously treated with a mixture of light oil and aloe tincture (aloe medicinalis) could create similar decolourations as seen on the Shroud, as a result of the decomposition of chemical particules of human sweat into ammonium vapours that action a process of oxydation in the cellulose of the material. This colouration is strongest where the tissue touches the body and weakens, consequently, with the distance of the linen from the body. This explains quite perfectly why the body-copy corresponds to photographic negative. Professor Vignon declared that the picture-print on the cloth had materialized mainly through ammonium vapours which the body liberated through emanation of feverish, uric-acid sulphure. With these substances, the solution of aloe and myrrh drenched in the tissue would have reacted, building up ammonia-carbonate which vapours did decolour towards darkness the fibres of the cloth in the humid atmosphere between skin and linen with direct proportionality to the contact with the body.

The clearly darker colouration of the blood stains derives from a stronger chemical reaction. That in occasion of the apparent funeral a rather suspiciously large quantity of aloe and myrrh had been employed, has been mentioned in the gospel by John: '...he (Joseph of Arimathiaea) now went (to Golgotha, coming from Pilate) and operated the deposition (of Jesus) from the Cross. But also Nicodemus who ha come the first time by night to visit Christ, appeared and brought a mixture of myrrh and aloe, about one hundred pounds (around 40 kg presumably). They took the body of Jesus and wrapped it, together with the spices, in linen bandages, as it is the custom with the Jews, and burried it'.

The actually quite convincing arguments of Professor Vignon met with very harsh critics in the year 1933, because for the proposed chemical reaction there would have been necessary body salts and minerals, and bodily warmth, to obtain such an evaporation, but these factors could not have been present in sufficient concentration - with a corpse. Nevertheless, it had been proved now that a simple mixture of myrrh and aloe, applied in a humid and warm ambiance, could really produce undestroyable body prints on tissues. Examinations would show that even a very short period of contact of such a mixture with tissues, of 45 seconds only, could already lead to feable prints which could supply, from a photographic negative on the cloth, a clearly visible positive picture. With the explanation of the vaporisation theory one could have renounced on any further speculations. But - and this was the argument of the church -jewish corpses are invariably washed before the funeral and that, consequently, blood stains on the Shroud were impossible and, furthermore, that corpses do not sweat and cannot emanate any kind of warmth. Since, however, the body print pictures in the Shroud are irrevocably there, logic tells that wrapped in the Shroud in the antichamber of the grave there lay a body still alive, warm and sweating whereby a quite high temperature evolved as a result of beginning wound-fever and the tossic body emanations caused by the liquid on the sponge at the Cross. The inevitable conclusion is:

JESUS WAS FACTUALLY BURRIED ALIVE

A final examination of those factors that speak for the genuineness of the Holy Shroud of Turin would read as follows:

1) - The existence of a complete travel biography of the linen of Christ, starting on Easter sunday of the resurrection at Jerusalem with the note in the apocryphical gospel of the Hebrews: ...then he (Jesus) went to his brother Jacobus, after having given over his grave linen to the 'servant of the priest'. (Stations: Damascus, Edessa, Konstantinopel until 1204 post, Roussillon (southern France), Cornwall (Britain) during the Hundred Years war with France, then Lirey near Troyes (France), Chambéry (France), Turin in Piemont (Italy).

2) - The very rare weaving mode of the Shroud: it is a linen tissue, namely a twill in the very extraordinary and expensive legation 3:1, which means that under the vertical warp threads there are always three horizontal shot threads. Such an advanced weaving technics was not possible in Europe before the end of the 14th century and can nowhere be proved before the 16th century, and even then, it was always very seldom.

3) - The discovery of flower pollen of no less than 58 different plant species, out of which only 17 are original of France and Italy where the Shroud had been hidden as proved by its history ever since the 14th century. All other plant pollen sorts originate in the Middle East, some in Turkey, but no less than 44 species are typical for the flora of central Palestine and Syria. Many of them are halophyts that can grow only on hea- vily salty ground (desert areas).

4) - The NASA and scientifics' definite proof of human blood on the Shroud, without slightest trace of colour, chemicals, oxydations, etc. And the proof that on the grounds of having found serum halos around the blood stains, living blood must have trickled into the linen. The body of Jesus came, however, into contact with this linen only after his demise and deposition from the Cross.

5) - The total absence of any trace of decomposition of the body in the Shroud, after nearly 36 hours of closest body contact withe the alleged corpse. Then, the death-catalepsy (rigidness) would not have allowed to enter the narrow passage of the tomb chamber entrance with extended arms from death on the Cross, without ungearing the shoulder articulations to put his arms and hands crossed over his ado-

men, as the picture print on the Shroud would reveal.

6) - The cauterization of the linen by means of the chemical reaction of the myrrh-aloe compound, by uric-acid (ammoniac formation) transpiring through the pores of the skin, in conjunction with sweat and body warmth. All this could be proved in the laboratory. Colours instead would have drenched the thissue, not corroded the thread points only as it is the case with the Shroud.

7) - In this manner there evolved literarily a photographic negative, with sides and dark/clear nuances exchanged, roughly 1850 years before the invention of photography at all! And only because this is really a negative picture it was possible to extract from the print on the linen a three dimensional picture (see Christ's original features on the booklet-cover), a fact that would have been technically im-possible to extract from a painting.

8) - The cloth could be plied in a way that only the visage of Christ appeared on a quadrangle. This picture was now copied in painting a thousand times, portraying it with a circled or oval frame like a medallion in the antique Roman manner. Thus took birth the art of producing Icones in the east. And out of the latin word combination 'vera icona' (genuine Icone) was developped the story of the sweat-cloth or Sudarium of one of the mourning women, named 'Vero-nica'.

9) - The portrait on the linen was evidently known to early Christianity. There is little doubt that the fatally wrong decision of the deification of Christ at the concilium of Nicaea, 325 post under the Roman emperor Constantine the Great was heavily influenced by the existence of this 'mischievous' picture (Mandillion). Because, who else than God in person would be able to leave to humanity as remembrence of his presence on earth in the flesh a complete portrait of his visage and body on his mortuary linen?

10) - The Shroud of Turin pictures a whole series of bloody wounds which had not been reported in our sacred scriptures, nor could they have been ever known, such as:

a) - The broken nasal bone that must have handicaped respiration on the Cross considerably and might have been co-responsible for the early collapse on the Cross.

b) - The greatly swollen right cheek and other facial injuries that resulted from the crash on the floor of Via Dolorosa on the way to Golgotha, and from inflicted strokes.

c) - The heavy scorial injuries of the skin on the left shoulder that resulted from the carrying of the heavy wooden patibulum (the horizontal wooden block for the Cross), that was tied behind his neck on to both arms. It has been argued that the shoulder injuries could have been caused by the point of the spear that had been plunged in the hanging body on its right(!) side, between the 5th and 6th rip. This is sheer non-sense. The point of the spear, more than half a meter in length, would have had to be pierced right through Christ's entire thorax, out of a quite impossibly narrow angle from the ground, not to speak of the impossibility to withdraw such a spear without causing horrible mutilations of the body that would have been reported with certainty by the eyewitness disciple John in his gospel. Instead he says: ...and immediately after the spearpoint-thrust blood and water emerged. A wound then it was, not a total penetration of the body.

d) The 21 x 2 flagellation strokes that do appear on the Shroud. Nobody had ever known so far the exact number of whip-lashes received by Christ.

e) - The current of blood on the cloth that demonstrates that at first the left arm was freed from the nail, then the right arm, from the patibulum. And that the wounds caused in the scalp by the crown of thorns started to bleed only after the deposition from the Cross, so to speak 'post mortem', which would not have been possible with a lifeless body.

f) - The complete absence of any trace of decomposition of the corpse in the linen, after closest contact with it over nevertheless about 36 hours.

g) - The discovery of the two money pieces, both coined in the years 28-29 post under Pilate that could be recognized as very feable photographic prints, only possible thanks to most modern technology, and which had been put on Christ's eyelids in occasion of his burrial by perons who had been, evidently, left in the believe that Jesus had died - while other persons present would know better...

And as mentioned before, even the years of coinage of these pieces is now known, namely some three years before the drama on Golgotha.

One can easily see: The proofs for the genuineness of the Holy Shroud of Turin are quite overwhelming and can hardly be contradicted in any point.

In addition to the above, we may reconsider the most evident arguments why this Shroud can n o t possibly be a medieval fake, a circumstance that has meanwhile been accepted and confirmed also by the Vatican itself, since february 1991:

A) - The Templer order of Jerusalem had been founded on the secret knowledge of the Shroud and was thus persecuted by the Catholic Church and the Kingdom of France until its final annihilation, with the accusation to 'venerate and pray to a face' - precisely to the visage of the Mandilion. But already in 1204 post the French cruisade knight, Robert de Clary, discovered the mysterious and accurately guarded Shroud inside the chapel of Saint Mary of Blacherne, in Constan-tinopolis, then capital city of the Eastern Roman empire (nowadays Istanbul on the Bosporus), in occasion of the sack of the city by christian (!) Venicians, and brought it on clandestine ways, via Hungary and Besançon, to southern France. This occurred still at least 150 years earlier than any alleged artifice or falsification.

B) - Only a maniac or otherwise mentally ill artist could have thought of painting a tortured and disfigured, naked male body, photonegatively inversed, in gray tones, with blood stains and coagulated blood clods everywhere, in particular also at places that had never before been reported by tradition and were thus entirely unknown. What, however, taking up the challenge, would have been required from an imaginary artist of the 14th century?

For once, a perfecct knowlege of the human anatomy - which was not possible before the advent of Leonardo da Vinci. The man in the Shroud can only be recognized at a distance of at least 1-2 meters. But an artist cannot paint when not seeing the effect of his brush strokes. Since a lot of single fibres with a diameter of 10-15 micron had to be slightly touched or drenched, a brush of 1-2 meter's length would have been re-quired, with only one single bristle of sable hair(!) which, compared with the linen fibres, would still have been too thick, because the seen colour would actually trickle into the tissue, just as real blood does.

Furthermore, the artist would have needed a binding material containing neither oil nor water as absolutely no capillarity is discernable in the linen. He would have had to paint with blood, with real living blood, and he would have needed a microscope of considerable focus in order to see what he was actually painting. This relates to the blood stains and traces. Quite contrary were the situation regarding the outlines of the body and its actual printed reproduction. Here, the tissue fibres show only singes at their tips and thus at the surface of the linen, as a result of the described chemical reaction. In analogy with the the blood stains, a presumed artist would have had to touch the surface of the shroud only extremely lightly, hardly exhaling, with an equally superfine brush, in order to avoid that the colour drenched the fibres and trickled into the tissue.

A further consideration would be the limited human nervous system. Nobody could possibly hold a brush, or any other instrument, without lightly trembling long enough to only dab or dot single tissue fibrillas. The artist would have had to know exactly how many fibrillas he had to dab, and the whole painting would have had to be done with inverted sides and colouring, like a negative, otherwise we would not be able to obtain to-day a positive photography out of the linen - which we do. In order to mark the lashes of flogging, serum albu-mina would have been needed. This feature, however, is only recognizable in ultraviolet light. And if taking up the hypothe-sis that the portrait could be a result of oxydation, one would have had to paint it with sulphuric acid (!) which would have destroyed the brush bristles and corroded the linen.

It became inevitably clear: the GENUINENESS of the Holy Shroud of Turin cannot be contradicted. This, then, signifies ultimately that Christ had survived the Cross. And if this is true - then the history around Christ's earthly life must have a continuation - somewhere. We shall hint at it in the next chapters of this abridged publication and explain it in all details in the coming main books, in a three-volumes narrative, and, in addition, a comprehensive book of facts, divided into two segments: The book of doubts, and the book of proofs.

With this discovery a greater surprise for the history of christianity, basing on to this day only on the four gospels, the apostolate history by Luke and Saint Paul's letters, cannot be avoided. But then this new and dramatic knowledge will also have the beneficial effect of clearing so many highly enigmatic passages in the New Testament - and finally - free christianity from many doubts and nightmares that resulted from that far away, strange Easter sunday morning happenings at an empty tomb and allow the christian churches to get rid of childrens' shoes, step out of religious puberty and become, after two thousand years of hindrances, really grown up.

*

15. The revolutionary interpretation of Crucifixion

The apparent misinterpretation of the events after the Cross by Saint Paul was, however and at the same time, a masterly achievment in spiritual history. It has been Pul who really and entirely kindled the fire Christ had come in this world to lit up. Paul must have thoroughly known after the encounter with Jesus resurrected in Damascus that he had not gone on the Cross to die in penitence for the sins of this world. Those were ideas of visibly hellenistic character and which did not nearly comply with jewish religious attitudes. But he, Paul, could not possibly spread out with success that Jesus had tried to challenge God himself on Golgotha to descend down and accredit him in front of his nation, but that he had failed in great part. Furtermore, it was in those times by no way sure that Jesus had really died and had been resurrected a short while thereafter since the criteria about transition from life to death were different from those of to-day, and by far less exact and reliable. Then, the absolute standstill of respiration was considered as total lifelesness. This, then, did presently match the case of Jesus.

Nowadays medicine, however, knows that survival can be possible not only in spite of ceased respiration, but also with ceased heart-beating. Later, in the middle ages, the standstill of the heart was officially considered as state of death. We must, then, not stumble over this technological progress achieved over twothousand years. Paul, and with him also Jesus, were quite entitled to assume that death had actually occurred and that the miracle of a resurrection from death had taken place. This phenomena had, however, the flaw that Jesus had to return to his previous, earthly life, his body covered with painfull injuries everywhere, and not trans-figured as fervently hoped. And without the slightest proof of a miraculous divine intervention by the Father himself. Then, it is evident, that during his deathlike coma in the grave, Jesus had had no dreams, nor did he view the paradise, nor hear angels' trumpets, nor did he hear God's voice explaining to him the sense of these strange events.

All this is very significant and has to be read - between the lines of our four gospels - what so far has hardly been dared. At the same time, we are allowed to imagine the great dilemma of Jesus himself: He had expected a clear YES or NO to his self-interpretation by God; he had tried to live the life of a God-pleasing saint. To combat misery on earth, to preach goodness for the glory of the Heavenly Father, and to prepare the coming-down on earth of the Celestial Kingdom of God. At the same time, for all events, to fulfill to the letter all prophesies of the jewish Scriptures, to make it possible for God to confirm him in the one or the other of his possible roles to play - just as it would please the Allmighty.

*

16.God denies Christ's sacrifice - but acts salvation

And now, the Allmighty does not accept the voluntary sacrifice of the Son of Man, he repulses him into his earthly existence, without the official legitimation so intensely hoped for. Once more, Jesus finds himself all alone and compelled to try to interpret the actual will of God for him, out of the current events. It's Saint Paul then who realizes that the scriptures of the prophets had been entirely fulfilled, that the suffering servant of God had really been spared and saved in a miraculous way by the Celestial Father, and that he himself was standing, at Damascus, before the resurrected and living Messiah and priestly king of Israel.

These circumstances decided the basic teachings of the Resurrection with western christianity , but the theology of salvation of the entire mankind on the Cross hardly stems from Christ himself but can be seen as a genious inspiration by Saint Paul and his environment, basing on the spontaneous exclamation of young John, the beloved disciple, in front of the empty tomb on that Passah morning in Jerusalem: ...'Christo resurrexit!' (the Lord has arisen!).

Paul has shown considerable capacities by converting a great resignation and threatening defeat into a splendid victory in virtue of the alteration of the motive of the crucifixion in a hellenistic sense, and to the presentation of the phenomena of the resurrection in a manner understandable to the Greek mentality, rather than the Jewish, giving it a real and fair chance for acceptation among the hellenistic people of the Middle East.

Without this rather fantastic idea of Christ doing penance on the Cross for the entire humanity for the final foreigveness of all sins, it would have resulted quite impossible to propagate the new moral and new ethics of non-violence by loving your neighbours, even your enemies, with so much success in the whole Roman empire.
The new teachings had received their uncomparable and exotic labels and packing. And on the etiquettation and way of presentation of the new doctrine depended all and everything:

in Antiochia, in Lyddia, in Gallatia, in Corinth, in Ephesus and later also in Rome. The entire early christian church history is drenched by this altered lead-motif of the Son of God who had died on the Cross for the sins of the world, had been resurrected and soon afterwards elevated to Godfather up in the skies.

Once the ship had been tugged out of the port, gained the open sea and proved seaworthy, tugs are no longer needed. In exactly the same way it is high time to get rid of so much ballast of unhistorical beliefs which have most powerfully prevented christiandom and its supreme teachings from any form of emancipation. Christ was not at all intent on sacrificing himself for the sake of humanity's sins, but was desperately directed to finding the final truth on his own mission for, at first judaism, then for humanity on the Cross, in the face of God and death. He had decided to challenge God and obtain his visible legitimation as his representative and envoy in the fight against unjustice, poverty, evil and despair, illness and suffering, and the satanic powers of darkness, and for the forces of light in this world.

But he could not but fail, because God could not possibly act against his own will, his own creation and natural order and oppose himself in favour of one of his creatures. Because not only the heavens and paradise, but also the hells are God's own creations and dominions. Day and night condition each other, as does good and evil, in a perpetual equilibrium, but the latter phenomena do not at all exist in nature. And while we have made it a habit to transvest the evil, giving it the appearance of good, we can no longer distinguish the one from the other and are falling currently victim of evil camouflaged and clad as virtue and 'good'.

Christ could not break the divine laws of the dualistic forces in this world. But with his truly heroic deed and with the help of Pauline tactics he actually did reach the most impressive goal of enhancing the signification of the spheres on the positive side for human life and lay the cornerstone for a more social, somewhat brighter, less hungry, less poverty-striken and more festive and less frustrated world.

*

17. Pentcost - A coronation without the king...

It is quite evidently Jesus of Nazareth in person, physically returned into his old and previous earthly life who does appear to his disciples on their way to Emmaus and at the shores of lake Genezareth in Galilee, as clearly mentioned in all christophanic reports of the gospels. Because of his complete disguise they seem to be unable to recognize their Rabbi in the darkness and twilight of burning candels and torches at their secret house of hiding in Jerusalem; they are overcome with doubts that he be it really - but it is him, truly and incarnate. And even while still recovering from his traumatization and corporal wounds, Christ starts forgeing new plans. He actually does prepare his emigration. To his loyal disciples he implies the renewed order of baptism. And he sanctions the propagation of his new teachings and missioning amongst the heathen populations of the Greek world and within the Roman empire. He sets the cornerstone for the foundation of the first jewish-jesuanic (christian) communities and the consequent church.

He has drawn the lots among his twelve disciples, for them to be sent out for missioning in different countries (after a stay of 12 years in Jerusalem), whereby Thomas drew the lot 'India', aginst which he first opposes for a long time, but eventually accepts his fate. And Christ has Peter (Simon) presiding over the jesuanic community at Jerusalem. He contrives to impart to the jewish crop-thanks-giving (Scha'wuot) festivities of Pentcost (50 days after Passah) the entirely new signification of the symbolic descent of the Holy Spirit on the heads of his community. And with Christ, unseen in the background, he arranges for the ritual of the foundation act of his Ecclesia, the christian church of the coming centuries, by having Peter read out the new gospel in the name of the Resurrected One, in all possible languages in those days spoken by the population and festivity visitors in Jerusalem. Thus the biblical mention: ...and suddenly they, Christ's disciples, spoke in many different tongues... . - Jesus himself is silently absent at his own coronation (or that of his teachings) and, strange enough, also Mary of Magdala is missing at the congregation. But his mother Mirjam, and his (half-)brothers mark their presence, representing Jesus, even though until the events on Golgotha scepticism had prevailed, particularly from his brothers. Now, everything pepared for letting the seed grow, Jesus has to flee and leave Roman dominated territories - as we know, for ever.

*

18. Death to the world ....

Jesus deeply deplores having to leave as he loves his country and his homeland Galilee in which he is profoundly rooted. Except for Egypt, he has never dwelt for longer in a foreign country. He now directs his steps, in great secrecy, to near Damascus in Syria, then not Roman dominated and where already long ago a jewish-essenic community had been established. There, he will be hiding, for about 1 1/2 years - the apocryphic gospels mention 560 days. On taking leave from his disciples in occasion of the so wounderfully described scene on Mount of Olives by the evangelist Luke, facing the sturdy city walls and the glorious Herodian temple of Jerusalem, he says: '...There, where I am going, you cannot follow me'. His disciples do know that their Rabbi is still among the living, but with time passing by, they slowly lose him out of sight. Nevertheless, he did promise on to them to return. This was actually his intention, as soon as the political situation in Palestine would alter, or tension remarkably diminuish. But destiny has other events in store for him. At Jerusalem, all signs of the political barometer tend towards stormy times.

Four years after crucifixion, in the same spring of 36 post (AD), Pontius Pilate as well as the president of the great Synhedrium, the supreme high priest Joseph Kaiphas, are removed from their respective offices and functions. Pilate, accused of a massacre in Samaria is banished to Gallia, and Kaiphas has to step down for his too good relations with the Roman governour - ever since Golgotha may be?

*

19. Pilate's bones on a peak in Central Switzerland?

Pontius Pilate will die a prisoner in Rome although there exists another version telling that he had been sent into banishment to Gallia (France), to the city of Vienne (south of Lyon), where he had expired. Centuries later, his bones were dug up by christians (in Rome?) who apparently felt harrassed and tormented by his ghost, and thrown into a dark little lake on top of Mons Pilatus near the nowadays city of Lucerne in Central Switzerland, at Roman times a northern province of wilderness of the empire, void of inhabitants, and therefore called 'the woodlands of the alps'. - The ascent of this cursed mountain peak of some 2500 m (about 7800 feet), towering high above the Four-Woodlands-Lake, had been forbidden on death penalty by the catholic church authorities until the middle of the 19th century.

At Jerusalem, king Agrippa I dies in the year 44 post (AD). Peter (Simon) passes his leadership of the jewish-christian communities to Jacobus Justus (James the Just), the true oldest half-brother of Jesus in the flesh, son of Mary and Joseph (or of whose brother Clophas-Alphaeus). He himself directs his steps towards Rome, probably via Antiochia and the hellenistic cities of Asia Minor. In the year 62 post Jacobus Justus, who meanwhile had become High Priet at the Herodian Temple (!), is being led on the temple roof, pushed over the city wall down into the Kidron valley below and, still alive, brutally clubed to death. The mere and astonishing fact that Jesus' oldest brother takes over a priestly kingdom in the function as (royal) High Priest, though in a less accentuated manner since the Romans are still the masters of Palestine as usurpators, does strongly underline the thesis of pretention to the throne of Israel, first by John the Baptist, then after him by Jesus. The royal title was evidently at stake and in the game. The crown of thorns for Jesus was not wound for mere fantasy, but did have an earnest political background and significance.

Jesus of Nazareth, now bodily and physically handicaped, cannot show himself again to the people of Judea. His injuries, symbols of his -apparent- defeat on the Cross, would have been seen as a denial of his alleged legitimation which he had pretended, before Golgotha, as Son of Man, or Son of his Father in the heavens. And after the Last Supper and with-out the slightest hint to his disciples and his family of a possible return, or even a resurrection from the death, his environment reacts greatly surprised - and only hesitatingly pleased. Jesus, who had foreseen all and everything con-cerning his own ordeal and execution, had not pre-told his possible survival inspite of respective plans and preparations, for justified fear that these could be inarbitrarily betrayed. Therefore,his disciples prove considerable difficulties in belie-ving in Christ's physical return.

But then Jesus manages to persuade his disciples of the will of God and proves on to them that he has literaly fulfilled all the inherent prophesies in the holy scriptures of the Old Testament and related them to his person. Jesus convinces not only his immediate followers, but also his brethren (four in number) who had stood off and in opposition to him before the Cross. They now believe in the prophesies of Jesaia about the Messiah who had foretold that the Suffering Servant of God must survive the ordeal.
*

20. The decisive days of Damascus

In Damascus, Christ prepares his emigration to the East. He himself has to renounce on any activity within the border lines of the Roman empire as he is still a wanted fugitive. If he were arrested again he would suffer death penalty a second time. What he now needs is a herold of great capacities and talents, to carry the message of the New Alliance into the Wet and the graeco-roman world.

At this point, a man named Saulus emerges, in occasion of the stoning of the very first christian martyr, Stephanus, diacon of the earliest christian community in Jerusalem. Although Saul's task is to supervise the execution of Stepha-nus, he is highly impressed by the composedness, eloquence and faithfulness to the new creed in the face of imminent painful death. Saul becomes strangely contaminated and full of curiosity. He wants to get to know the extraordinary person that was Christ. From the Synhedrium, highest religious authority and tribunal of the Jews, he obtained a letter of accreditation imparting to him authority of travelling with a suit of solders to Damascus. And why then, if he had not known whom to meet there? It would have been far simp-lier to chase and persecute Jesus' disciples who were still hiding in Jerusalem, all of them - than a possibly transfigured ghost...

In thouse weeks, Saulus, a young student of jewish laws and already a member of the said Synhedrium, a sort of Jewish National Assembly comprising 72 members, had suffered a great personal deception: he had asked in marriage a daugh-ter of the supreme high priest (Kaiphas?), but was rebuffed, for unknown reasons. He might thus have nurtured the idea of an expedition to Damscus, and turn his back to Jerusalem for a while to forget his chagrin.

But the meeting was, obviously, arranged for, and Jesus is perfectly aware of Saul's arrival. And once again we are witnessing the geniality and the dramaturgic vein of Christ: He does not simply await his fate, but acts by surprising Saul on the road, some distance out of Damscus. Saul, then converted to Christ and with his new name Paul, will tell the story of his strange encounter with the Risen One later at least four times, in ever different ways.

Saul falls on the ground, stricken by blindness for several days, after having seen Jesus in his long white robe and after having spoken to him. Jesus let him conduct into Damascus, to a man of his confidence, a certain Ananias, who would re-store Saul's eyesight in the next days. Is it possible that he was offered a beverage, perhaps even by someone out of his own suit?

Was there again the juice of the swallow-root, the narcotic soma brew or that of the tossic Sodom apple in the game, like with Lazarus, like on Golgotha? Or, perhaps, another drug? Should Saul not know the exact location where he was brou-ght to in Damascus, and lose his orientation for some time?

Or do we have to interprete the narration in a symbolic way, assuming that Saul had been stricken with blindness hithertoo while persecuting the early christian communities and that he had now been lead on the way of ultimate truth by the great Nazarene, becoming 'seeing'?

Whatever the truth: At the gates of Damscus in Syria Saul encounters the resurrected and incarnate Jesus of Nazareth-and takes also to the new faith. He is re-baptized Paul, a name change to which he was entitled biy his Roman citizenship. He will prove the required recipient and leader and the ideal instrument for promulgation of the new Jesuanic Gospel in the West. Here in Damascus, the tremendous power of conviction of Jesus on Paul will lead to the first, yet still unseen, blows to the mighty Roman empire, weakening it over the centuries by the new doctrine of non-violence and contributing thus to the final fall and destruction of the Empire in the West.

*

21. Christ and Paul divide the Unseen Realm

The division of the then known world into two great spheres for religious conquest takes place. Paul, a brillant orator and infinitely better educated than the original twelve disciples, zealous, both of tough nature in warding off punches and imparting such, of both Jewish and Roman nationality, should prove successful in what Christ would never have achieved: To transmit, save and transfer the great truths of jesuanic ethics and the nucleus of the sermon on the Mount over to our time and generations. For this uncomparable merit, we owe gratitude to Paul for ever.

Even though he had kept a secret some to us quite important details on Christ Resurrected. Even though he had, rather in opposition to Jesus' attitude which was clearly positive to human joys in life, put chains of an excessive puritanism on it causing infinite damage with his own depreciation of women and matrimonial links. And even though he had substituted, for the coming generations right down to us, the creed i n Jesus for the creed o f Jesus.

Christ for his part had realized that his hiding in Damascus had been discovered, that this city was no longer sure for him. He would have to take up his flight once more. Only the East was not dominated by the Romans. Only in the East the Ten Lost Tribes of Israel could possibly be found. It will, therefore, be in the East where we shall have to look for and discover the Second life of our Jesus Christ.

*

THE UNKNOWN, SECOND LIFE OF JESUS CHRIST

22. Christ resurrected on his way to the East

Eventually, Jesus received an invitation from king Ukama IV (called: the Black One) from Edessa in the south-east corner of nowadays Turkey, in areas of kurdish peoples, to visit and heal him from a malicious illness. The Rabbi from Nazareth had had answered him that he would have to fulfil his duty for which he had been sent and borne but would have delegated his disciple Thaddeus to the king to heal him. This, then, happened, and Thaddeus proved successful. In later years, also Christ's apostle Thomas (possibly Thaddeus' father) appeared at king Ukama's court in Edessa. Jesus, however, could never travel to Edessa as Paul's emissarie had already sent word to his kingdom that the Master had died, was resurrected from the dead and ascended to heaven.

Could he then surprise the people by his personal appearance, post mortem, in flesh and blood? Quite impossible. It would seem that St. Thomas achieved to christianise the kingdom of Edessa, which at times belonged to Armenia, completely before undertaking his voyage to India. Centuries after St. Thomas death, his bones were taken from south India (Mylapore, Madras) to Edessa for his final burrial.

The great migration does start, presumably, in the autumn of the year 33 post. Christ wanders at first to Nyshibin, a neighbouring city of Edessa but which, contrary to this latter, was not tributary to the Romans, but to the Persian Parths and stayed under their hegemony. There, we hear of an upheaval caused by Jesus and which did compel him to flee from the city, as so many times before. We encounter him next in the capital city of Arbela, in the adjacent kingdom of Adiabene at the upper Euphrates stream (also situated in nowadays' Kurdhistan in northern Iraq). Adiabene's royal family seems to have proselitized to the mosaic faith and to have been a remote family relationship of Jesus' great parents on mother Mary's side, over queen Helena of Adiabene who did have her own villa at Jerusalem, in the Ophel quarter, south of the great temple. There, Jesus finds a new exile and hiding place until the year 44 post (AD) when king Itzates, son of Helena, is murdered and Christ must flee again, in the direction of the mountainous Partherland Persia, to the East.

From now on, the Nazarene changes his name to Yuz, the persion version of Jesus (or Jehoshua), and eventually he was called Yuz Asaph which could be translated with 'the gatherer'. Collector of leprous people and other illness stricken patients looking for their healing, as some researchers believe. Or, alternatively, it could mean the collector of the Lost Ten Tribes of Israel in the East which would definitely make more sense. But, much more likely, it refers to a 3 m long, metal-pointed stick of olive wood, to support his walking and defence against wild biests. The arabs will call Yuz by the name of Isa, Issa or Issana. Which is what he is called in the holy Coran, up to this day.

The search for the Lost Tribes of old Israel in the East was, then, the yet unaccomplished part of the mission Christ had come into this world for, according to his own statements on several occasions, as reported in our New Testament. Jesus wanders now through the mountainous region of Iran as far as the city of Mashed in eastern Persia, to the tomb of Noah's son Sem, whose races of succession we call to-day semitic, which is true for both Hebrews and Arabs.

During long four years Jesus takes a dangerous passage through Iran and Afghanistan, together with his mother Mary who had never been in Ephesus, to-day on Turkey's western Aeghean coast. Inspite of the contrary vision of the german order-sister Catharina Emmerich (1774-1824), who saw Mary's hous of demise in a dream above Ephesus. John, Christ's beloved disciple to whom he had entrusted the care of his mother from the Cross, went to Ephesus only at the time of the great Roman-Jewish war. This happened around the year 66 post. By that time, Mary would have been 88 years old as she was 16 at the time of Jesus' birth-and that had been in the year 6 ante (BC=before Christ). Also Mary of Magdala, who according to the apocryphic gospel of Philippus, one of the original disciples of Jesus, travels with the party. Thomas, who at first refused his lot drawn for India, was sold in Mesopothamia to a merchant of a king in India according to a very strange story told in the Acts of Thomas, was then made to sail to Sindh (Pakistan), at the court of a king Gondophares, in north-west India. In the greek-hellenistic capital city called Taxila, at the foot of the prealps to the Himalayas, we find these four personalities of paramount importance in our religious traditions again united. Together, they take part in a royal marriage at the kings' court, around the year 48 post (Christian calendar).

*

23. Christ, Mary, Magdalena and Thomas in India

Shortly thereafter we read about a great military invasion jof armies of the Scyths who overran the defenseless plains of north-western India. Mary the mother, Magdalena and Jesus take again to flight, into the hilly country north of Taxila, on the road to the old and beautiful valley of Cashmere, the real 'Promised Land' of the Old Testament which even bears, up to to-day, an ancient hebrew name, the land of 'Cash'. But on the way to Cashmere, mother Mary dies, in a mountain village only some 40 km out of Taxila (to-day near Islamabad-/Rawalpindi, capital of Pakistan), high above the hot Indian plains, and is being burried at Pindi Point in a village still called Muree (Mary!), in her remembrance. Even at the time of British occupation her tomb was still venerated by the village folks who even prevented its removal by the British military who wanted to construct a radio tower on that site.

Thomas, to the contrary, sailed down the Indus river and took sail to South India, to the Malabar coast (to-day's Kerala), to mission amongst the colonies of the so-called 'Black Jews',for more than 20 years. Later, he went over to south India's east coast, to the Coromandel country were he was unintentionally killed, near Mylapore (to-day: Madras) by the arrow of a brahmin priest chasing a bird, according to written traditions around the year 68 post (the Roman emperor Nero died in the same year in Rome). These are already historically ascertained facts. St. Thomas' mortal remains were transferred to Edessa in Armenia as early as the 4th century AD and, as already told, re-burried there definitely, while his heart found a last resting place in a church in Umbria, Italy.

The gospel 'after Thomas', the so-called 'Thomas-Acts', and the numerous apocryphic writings and gospels from the very first century of christianity are most eloquent. Many Indian names, especially from among South India's royalties who had been converted by the apostle Thomas, are quite known. But also in that so remote country we come across the same difficulties as everywhere: collision course with the actual political authorities, request of renounciation of marital intercourse from the side of high rank and noble women towards their, often mighty, consorts, persecution of the converted, imprisionments, hearings under torture, admiration of martyrdom. Like in Asia Minor (Turkey). Like in Rome. In India, christian ideas could only reach the Parias, the 'Untouchables' who were not protected by caste, and could thus not have real success, as they did have a mighty enemy with the powerful gods of old India. Against this impressive pantheon, a crucified and suffering god could have not the slightest chances, except with the most miserable social layers.

Only to-day, after nearly 2000 years, christian thoughts and ethics are flowing visibly and strongly into antiquated Hinduism and are reaching, if by no means the masses, so more and more elitarious circles, writers, politicians, philosophers. Because the principles of non-violence, also preached by Buddhism over more than 2400 years, could prove a uniting factor that finds growing acceptance.

Even more so if it could one day be proved that the Krishna legends and the Vishnuan Bakthi-cults of India did have very old christian roots that stem from the areas of north-western India-where Lord Krishna was actually borne (at Mathura, between Delhi and Agra of to-day). The obvious similarity of the names of Krishna and Christ, both of ancient greek origines, have ever been striking.

*

24. Imperatif for correction-An order to the Church

Therefore, a fundamental correction becomes necessary in our days which had been overdue for centuries. The enormous, erratic rock of the Roman Catholic Church in the religious landscape has prevented any renewal. But it has also been this same church that preserved and saved the contents and the nucleus of the teaching of Christ, though altered, down to our generations and who has been, so far, the only world-wide christian organization to maintain and beware a compact unity, in obvious contrast to countless and utterly diversifying other churches, sects and denominations of christian beliefs.

This situation can be seen as a direct consequence of that stormy bishop-concilium of Nicea (western Turkey, city of Isnik to-day) in that remote year 325 post (AD), where the then Roman emperor Constantine the Great intervened among the heavily quarelling, mostly too young bishops (the elder elite had become victims of the christian persecutions under emperor Diocletian 295-298 post), who could not agree on their topic and decided, one time for ever, that Jesus Christ had been a true epiphany of God on earth, thus as Son of God, identic with the Father, 'homo-usios' in greek, (and not only 'homoi-usios' = similar to him), and that he has, therefore, divine attributions and capacities. This was quite in line with Jesus' self-interpretation.

Christ, then, according to the concilium of Nicea, had not only been a human of flesh and blood with divine inspirations as ascertained and believed by bishop Arianus of Constantinople, the syriac orthodox church and the kings of the German tribes of the Visi- and Ostro-Goths who had all embraced the Arian creed, in the knowledge of Christ's survival at the Cross, and his only apparent resurrection. Later it became necessary to make a definite choice among not less than 70 different gospels circulating in the christian communi ties of the first centuries, in order to cement and realize Christ's ultimate divinization. Whatever scriptures or gospels other than the four chosen canonical gospels of the Roman Catholic Church could be laid hands on where collected and destroyed, since any reports or allusions that could have put Constantine's verdict in question, could not be tolerated by the mighty catholic church.

Four gospels where thus selected to make up our New Testament, scriptures which did not present hints and stories contrary to Jesus' divine character and did thus best comply with the religious politics of Rome, and which had been fathered by authors that had either still known Christ personally, or at least one or more of his disciples or apostles. Only few alterations, or omissions, proved to be thus necessary.

For instance the cancellation and substitution of the very last paragraph of the gospel of Mark where quite obviously there must have been written something rather discriminating the growing belief in Christ's resurrection in the narrative of the events at the empty tomb.

The history of the young church, its steady growth and the creation and composition of our four canonical gospels (Mark, Matthew, Luke, John), as well as their publicity-complying tendencies, will be treated in special chapters. But also voluminous apocryphic literature, re-descovered and largely restored with great competence (Professors Hennecke-Schneemelcher), do open to our eyes very interesting, additional and new knowledge of the historical figure of Jesus and the personalities acting in his circles. There is, indeed, many a point that would have rendered our to-day's beliefs rather impossible.

A revision of the historical facts around the earthly life of the great Nazarene becomes both urgent and inevitable if we desire to contribute to restore the credibility of the christian faith for a large part of modern christians of our time, and for all those millions yet to be borne. So that we and they might be able to remain christians with faith, pride and dignity, in accordance with the discoveries of science and technology.

Only the revision of the fatal decision of Nicea, 17 centuries ago, would be necessary, and a clear transfer of significance from that mysterious early Easter morning of Passah, to the contents of the famous Sermon on the Mount, a new moral without blind obedience and to Christ's ethical teachings and great christian thruths found in the re-located Logias in the apocryphic gospel according to Thomas, undug in the Egyptian desert sands of Nag Hamadi, as late as 1947 post.

The magnificence of the 'Pater Noster' would shine unaltered also through the coming centuries and lose nothing at all of its mysterious attraction by a comparatively slight, yet most important move of the steering wheel.

*

25. Was, perhpas, Cashmere the 'Promised Land'?

There do exist quite a number of antique historical sources in Persian literature that do explicitly mention the passage of a religious personality namend Yuz Asaph, or Jehoshua, through the high plains of Iran and through to-day's Afghanistan. Equally, a great many authors have in the past taken up the subject of the Afghan-Pashtun tribes claiming their direct descent from the 'Ten Lost Tribes' of old Israel, who had been deported first from Palestine to Babylon, and later further to the East to Iran and north-west India, before and after the famous jewish captivity at Babylon (604-538 ante), under the kings Tiglat Pileser III and Sargon II, and still earlier after the occupation of Galilee (733 ante) and Samaria (722). The indices of an early settlement of the jewish race in the valley of Cashmere in north-wet India are so frequent that there remains little doubt about this historical circumstance. Not only are there up to this day hundreds of words, numericals as well as names of caste and persons, and also many geographical designations virtually identical to the letter in spoken cashmiri language with biblical denominations in ancient hebrew. The interesting table of comparison of the two languages by the indian writer Nazir Ahmad at the beginning of the 20th century shows a startling synonimosity which does lead to the conviction - that there in Cashmere, we are confronted with descendancy of the old jewish tribes.

Facial expressions, attire, colours of the skin; behavours of cashmiri people are so unlike to India, and of jewish tendency, like the legends and traditions of old. Some aspects seems surprising: As old jewish grave-sites, in an east-west direction, can be found in considerable numbers all over the country, and equally remains of possibly once hebrew synagogues or even tempels (Martand?) - but absolutely no hint at the mosaic religion or traditions. Such had been lost in those many centuries of migrations or, what would correspond to a new hypothesis, they had never been there! This could mean: The Bani (children) of Israel of the 'Ten Lost Tribes' of the history of the Old Testament had not settled anew in Cashmere in the 6th century ante (before Christ BC), but the hebrew race could have migrated from there to the west and Sumeria some thousand years before Christ, and before their Jahwe-beliefs professend by Abraham, later by the ancestor-patriarchs and, eventually, through Moses' Thora, came into existence! We may recall that Abraham fled out of the Sumerian capital Ur (southern Iraq) and nowadays Shat-el-Arab swamplands, near Basra and Kuweit, in the 18th century before our time.

The ancient hebrew calendar shows as equivalent to the solar year 1 post of the christian era the moon year 3694, without knowledge of even the erudated rabbinic circles of any historical departure point for their time-count.

The starting year could well have been the beginning of jewish emigration out of north-west India and the pre-alps of the western Himalayas - towards Mesopotamia, after the biblical Deluge or Great Flood (in german still called: Sintflut', whereby 'Sindh' was the old name of the Indus river, flowing through to-day's Pakistan.

In correlation to our solar calendar the year 1992 would have been equivalent to the jewish year 5558/9, also converted from moon years into solar years. If we now subtract the christian era from the hebrew year count, we do arrive at approximately the year 3586 before christ as the starting point of the jewish calendar in history. Interesting to note that jewish myths of the creation of the world and the chasing out of paradise mention an epoque of some 4000 years before Christ. And in that paradise there were apple trees, which did always exist in the cooler mountain climate of Cashmere - but never in India or in Mesopotamia.

New calendars have always marked important historical events in all ancient societies, for us the birth of Jesus Christ. It is a rather uneasy discovery that some of the old great prophets of Israel, like Ezechiel, Elia, Henoch and Moses, but also Jesus, whose tombs had never beenfound, had simply disappeared. And that they may have returned to the 'Pro-mised Land' of their forefathers - there to die. This reflection could lead to unexpected historical discoveries, far, far in the past.

*

26. The enigmatic tomb in Srinagar-city, Cashmere

In reality, not only the sepulchre of Jesus Christ has been rediscovered there, but also the last resting place of the biblical prophet Moses has been known for times immemorial in the valley of Cashmere. Strange enough, practically all the locality names related to the tomb of Moses and mentioned in the Old Testament and which were never found neither in Palestine nor in Transjordania, do exist in Cashmere. Even the name of this most northern state of India has hebrew roots: The country of the tribe of 'Cash'. Up to this day, numerous names can be found in Cashmere that present the syllable 'Yuz', in remembrance of Yuz Asaph, the fair-skinned prophet who came into the land from the far west, but also a 'stone' and 'a stick' of Moses that had also served Yuz Asaph, and moreover the 'ointment of Christ', sold until recent times on the markets in Srinagar, in addition to the heart-shaped paddles of the fishermen in the Dal-Lake which have their only counterparts on lake Genesareth in Galilee. It is quite impossible to believe in mere coincidence. All elements seem to resolve a puzzle: Jesus of Nazareth had decided, after the resurrection, to start his search for the Ten Lost Tribes of Israel, to quit the Roman dominated countries of the Middle East, and charge Paul with the missioning of the heathen in the west, to penetrate himself to the extreme east, to the fatherland of his ancestors, until Cashmere in north-west India. Christ's interpretation of his own role appears to have changed with time going on after the survival from crucifixion; the scarce evidence referring to utterings and speaches do rather indicate that he had definitely renounced on an identification as Messiah of Israel and as the Son of Man according to Henoch and that he had dedicated himself rather to an activity as healer, prophet and herold of his great Father-God in the heavens.

Such a choice and methamorphosis were of striking logic and necessity since he had found himself in areas with quite different beliefs: In Persia with the fire-cult of Zarathustra, in north-west India with Brahmanism, and in particular with early Buddhism, but also with idolatric cults of the most various kinds. The Essenic community of Qumran on the shores of the Dead Sea in Palestine did show clear connections with a very old Sun-God cult, and this aspect appears to hve gained weight again with Yuz Asaph in Cashmere when he meets, around the year 78 post AD, in the valley of Srinagar, the king of kings Shalesvahin to whose question what he were preaching, Yuz replied: 'Sire, my religion teaches love, truth and purity of the heart. It teaches men to serve God who dwells in the centre of the sun (!) and governs over the elements. God and the elements do last in eternity'. This is a part of a dialogue that has been reported and written down in an ancient book of the Hindus, called Bhavishya-Mahapurana, edited in the Laukika-year 3191 (corresponding to 115 post of the christian era. This would have been only eight years after the demise of Jesus at Srinagar (Surya-nagar = city of the Sun-God), in the year 107 of our time - Christ's own calendar! Since Jesus had been borne in the year 7 ante (astronomical count), he had died near Srinagar at the biblical age of 114 years of a natural death. The heavily damaged original of this sanskrit book (volume 8) is being kept and locked up under protection measures at the Institute of Oriental Researches of the Bombay University at Poona. But numerous photo publications are available.

The sepulchre proper lies in the midst of the old town of Srinagar, nowadays capital of Cashmere, at Khanyar-Street, is known as 'Rauzabal' and consists of a wooden structure of respectable size with inner rooms, a small ante-chamber, a small antique muslim cemetary by its side, the whole fenced with a wall and iron threads and was presumably built in the 14th century, over a far more antique tomb. A wooden sarco-phagus, covered with coloured clothes, stands over a rectan-gular stone plate under which there is a grave-chamber of not islamic origin, directed from east to west, hermetically sealed and to which up to now nobody has ever had access, nor was a permission to explore this strange grave-chamber ever given, neither by the states authorities of Cashmere or Delhi, India, nor by the islamic religious authorities of Srinagar. At the time when Cashmere was equally overran by the islamic-arabic armies like the rest of north-west India in the 13th century, this grave-site had, evidentially, been identified as the one of a great prophet of the sacred book, the personality of the prophet Issa who is also venerated in the holy Koran. Consequently, a remarkable islamic sanctuary had been erec-ted over this antique jewish grave. At the Rauzabal, there is an additional tomb of a believer of the prophet Issa (alias Jesus Christ), with the name of Sayid-Nasr-ud-Din. There is good reason to believe that he had been the architect, sponsor or founder of this very special memorial structure in the 14th century.

It will be remembered that prior to the advent of islam in Cashmere, earth burrial had no tradition, neither with the Buddhists, nor with the Hindus who, up to this day, practice almost exclusively cremation. But quite certainly, he Hebrews knew earth and stone burrials only. As a mater of fact, numerous ancient jewish graves have been located all over Cashmere. And Yuz Asaph's sepulchre does clearly bear jewish burrial marks. It had also been decorated with a tombstone rounded on the upper edge, as we still find them for example on the ancient jewish cemetary in the old town of Prague, Czecoslovakia. On the contrary, isalmic tombs are always directed in a south-westerly direction (seen from Cashmere), pointing with the head of the dead towards the holy city of Mecca in South Arabia.

It is an interesting circumstance that this sepulchre is in a fam ily's possession which is proved by a written verdict of a year

1766 post (christian era). The document bears the sig-nature of five mullahs and four judges (muffties) who do cert-ify in the document that this grave-site belongs to a holy prophet who had come from a far away country on the sea shores in the west some 1600 years ago and that the family was entitled, for ever, to dispose of any alms and gifts of charity presented to the sanctuary by (muslim) believers. To-day, it is an islamic grave-site which has received remarkable yet discret and silent publicity during the 20th century. Espe-cially in the eighties by numerous visits of foreigners and individuals, some times incognito, and particularly from Neo-Buddhist groups from France and other western countries. Muslim religious authorities in Cashmere did notice it with suspicion and have made efforts to encourage muslim in-habitants to re-frequent this sanctuary, sacrifice money and alms which did actually lead to a re-adjustment and cleaning of the building, providing, amongst other features, a brand new wallnut sculp-tered ceiling in the so typical cashmiri style, for the inner main room of the sanctuary.

There have been numerous attempts to obtain permission from the authorities to uncover and explore this mysterious tomb. But the government of India has so far declined all requests. Not only them. Also the catholic archbishop in Bom-bay, the then Monsignore Valerius, did deliberately reject any such project. It came to know that even the last British vice-roy for India, Lord Mountbatten, general in chief of the British Africa corps against Germany's general Rommel in Lybia and Egypt, during the Second World War, had paid a visit incognito to this strange sanctuary. Obviously because there is reason to believe that where there is smoke, there must also be fire.

The sequestration of pamphlets and booklets of Cashmiri writers in Srinagar's libreries and at the newspaper stand at the airport of the city, as well as a most curious inscription in pidgeon english at the sanctuary, itself pretending that 'all books so far written about this sepulchre are fake', do quite evidently nourish the suspicion that this sanctuary most be involved in some very enigmatic question. In an area that resembles anyway a steadily threatening volcano being bitterly contended frontierland between Muslim-Pakistan and

Hindu-India, and with Indian Cashmere showing a prevalently muslim population to-day, nobody can have an interest to kindle the fire with additional oil. Furthermore, the restless and quickly angry temper of the cashmiri populace who would not tolerate to lose one of their sanctuaries, even if for many centuries neglected, to the christians and foreigners, must be borne in mind. The foreseeable confrontation must be politically avoided - at the cost of a great truth. No new holy war, nor any sort of cruisade like the ones against Jerusalem in the 11th and 12th centuries are desired, as they would only open even more a wide gap again between muslim believers and adherents of the christian faith.

Moreover, it is highly unlikely that anything tangible could be found by unearthing the subterranean grave-chamber as it has probably been flooded time after time again by the ground-waters of nearby Dal-Lake. And if there were evidence uncovered, it would immediately disappear unpublished, since order and peace for the living are more important than the discovery of a bygone historical truth. The indices, how-ever, that Jesus of Nazareth lies burried in Cashmere are overwhelming, and the day ist to come where proofs will be available without opening the tomb. The religious history of Cashmere itself does furnish the clues and supports such attemps.

*

27. Yuz Asaph proclaims his prophethood, year 54

It was in the year 49 post that the local king of Cashmere, Gopananda (or Gopadatta), had taken over government and started his reign. This souvereign died in 109 post, that is two years after Christ. There are number of hints that already by that time a special sepulchre had been erected for a prominent messenger of God that was Yuz Asaph. In the year 54 post (christian era), king Gopananda ordered the re-stauration of the temple called 'throne of Salomo', situated on top of the hill Shankarcharyia, overlooking the city of Srinagar. As the king was evidently not a hindu (may be a buddhist), a certain 'Suleiman (or Sandiman) who stemmed from old Persia and may have been a liberal Jew, or Hindu, became a secretary to the king and was entrusted with the task. The prophet Yuz Asaph appears to have played an important role in the arbitration of a serious quarrel between hindus and buddhists over this very old sanctuary -of a jewish name! On one of the four restored pillars a strange message had been engraved: 'Yusz Asaph proclaims his prophethood, year 54. He is Yuz, of the Bani (children) Israel'.

This incision on the pillar-stone was still clearly legible at the time of the Moghul emperor Jehangir, around 1620 post, when the author Khwaja Haidar Malik Chadura wrote his history of Cashmere in 'The Tariki-Kashmir'. There are well preserved photographs of this inscription that has been, in the mean-time, plastered over, from the time of the British dominion of Cashmere at the beginning of the 19th century. Further al-lusions are the legends of Ladakh, the grave-site of Mary of Magdala near Kashgar in western China (Sinkiang province of to-day) -she is believed to have reached the age of 91-, as well as the burrial place of Mary, the mother of Jesus, at the mountain resort of Muree (Mary!) on the direct way from Taxila (Pakistan) into Cashmere (India). She would have died at the age of 76. Furthermore, the long wander- and defence stick made of olive wood, still preserved at Aish Muqam in the Srinagar valley and which, according to the legends, had first belonged to Moses, later also to Jesus. Where did it come from to Cashmere? There were no olive trees in India by that time.

*

28. Was Christ the Reformer of ancient Buddhism?

With some surprise it has been noted that the so-called 'Great Vehicle' of Buddhism, the Mahayana, emerged precisely in the 1st century Ad (after Christ) in the area of Cashmere and Ladakh and that from there it found its way via Nepal, Tibet, China, Mongolia and Corea as far as Japan were it became the origin of a new religious culture. In the year 78 post AD, thus in the same year where the prophet Yuz Asaph (alias Christ) met king Raja Shalesvahin, the important 4th Buddhist Con-cilium had been convened, with the erection of an appropriate palace, only some 12 km outside of Cashmer's early capital city of Srinagar and where for the duration of six months all 14th Buddhist schools of India deliberated about the possible schism of the Buddhist faith, into the great mainstreams, namely the 'Littel Vehicle' Hinayana, corresponding to the original and conservative teachings of the historical Gauthama Buddha, and the 'Great Vehicle' Mahayana, which seems to bear undeniable jesuanic traits that can hardly be overlooked even to-day. Again and again we are confused about apparent parallels in Buddhism and Christianity, particularly because the two great world-views do lie, theoretically, diametrically apart.

As a matter of fact, Buddha has virtually dethroned the Gods and abolished God as a supernatural power, seating on the highest throne over the universe the immanent world-law of the nexus of causality. Action provokes re-action. No dogmas. No creeds. As simple as that. Apparently. There is nothing, and nobody, and no gods caring about our personal fate. The universe knows nothing of our existence. We are swimming in a stream of laws and are being continously re-incarnated until we are successful, in a last of our countless existences, to annihilate our Kharma by total inactivity (doing neither evil nor good), attaining at the end the highest goal of destructing the vicious circle of metempsychosis and achieve extinction, thus entering Nirvana and giving thus our soul-substance back to the universe from which we had it once received. This is the nucleus of the Hinayana doctrine, renounciative and pessimistic in its general outlook. It would seem that this highest goal can only be attained by the Arhat, the self-disciplined monk, saddhu or eremite, with a scheduled life far from the stressed existence within human society. For the overwhelming majority of humans, and in particular for women, there is foreseen no salvation at all.

All this changes drastically with the appearance of Yuz Asaph in Cashmere where he will be active for another sixty years, including in the adjacent countries. Yuz Asaph preaches fervently his Fathergod 'Abba'(!), hebrew word for 'Father', and creates the Buddhist Fathergod Amith-Abba, the great Father of boundless light, whose centre is in the sun, who dwells in the heavens of the Western lands, in the 'Pure Land' -Paradise.It is an entirely new, never heard of religion of grace

It is sufficient to believe in Amithabba, no ascetic way of life, no sacrifices, no good works are necessary anymore (compare Christ's teaching in the New Testament: '..and none will come to the heavenly Father than through me!'). The success proves enormous. Now, and only now, Buddhism develops into a religion of the people, supported from the basis, what it had not been before. Suddenly, every human can attain salvation and strive for Paradise, especially also the women who had been almost completely locked out from the way to salvation by the orthodox system.

Is this not a profound jesuanic trait as we have seen the Nazarene again and again in his boundless compassion trying to mitigate the destiny of women and improve it in a strictly patriarchal society, like that of Old Israel? Much speaks in deed in favour of the hypothesis that Christ, alias Yuz Asaph, played an important role at the afore mentioned Concilium, possibly put in charge by the great king Kanishka of the Kushans, who had victoriously overran the entire north-west of India, who had ordered this 4th Buddhist Council and who, converting from Paganism to Buddhism, had taken a great interest in this philosophy. If this were historically true, the Nazarene would have introduced two paramount new aspects into Buddhism: for one thing the restauration of a highest supreme God in the heavens who would listen to personal needs and prayers and who would care for us (Amithabba), and then the command of brotherly love in the sense of limitless compassion. It is only from now on that the Great Vehicle Mahayana comes into existence and accepts the new and in Asia so extraordinary Divinity of Boundless Light and Compassion, in India called 'Avalokithesvara' (sanskrit term), in China 'Kuan-Yin', and in Japan 'Kwa-non'.

*

29. Was Christ the first Bodhisattva of Buddhism?

Yuz Asaph does create, out of himself, a new divinity: The Buddha Avalokithesvara, the Great Compassionate, the all-seeing divine Healer who, at the very moment of his own transition into Nirvana does not pass its threshold, renounces on the bliss of his own salvation, to remain at reach for the weak and wrecked of this world in all eternity, to help those miserable creatures too out of the stream of life, lifting them aboard the Great Vehicle of Mahayana and open to them the 'Pure Land', the paradise of the west, the realm of the supreme divinity of the light, Amithabba, and have their lost souls saved. What a grandious picture! The imagined heavenly 'Pure Land' lay in the west, seen from India, where Palestine is, or at the horizon of the sinking sun in the west, and later the original country of this new Buddhist doctrine was thought of springing from north-west India which, again, lies in the west seen from China or Japan. It is, indeed, almost impossible NOT to see the hand of Yuz Asaph, alias Jesus Christ, in this world-historic master deed of creating the Great Vehicle of Buddhism. Because contents of doctrine and teachings, the parables, the historic epoque and the locality of its advent do agree, correspond and harmonize in a so striking way that it would appear quite impossible to prove any valid counter argument to the above hypothesis.

Yuz or Jesus did create in the first century of our christian era the notion of the Bodhisattva (which stems from sanskrit, the classical liturgical language of antique India). The Bodhisattva is a great 'Just, Perfect and Enlighted One', a buddhist saint - who finds its counterpart withe the Hindus in their saddhus-, and who, in countless previous existences, has achieved, during his very last incarnation, to destroy his Kharma, being ready now to enter Nirvana, in order not to be reborne ever again. In Mahayana Buddhism there are as many Bodhisattvas as there are in the roman-catholic church, or many more. But there is a strange trait to the Bodhisattva: He does, and every new one does what Jesus of Nazareth had done: To try to reach God after having attained the highest human perfection to the state of sanctity and to quit this world voluntarily when the moment has come. But to renounce, at the decisive moment of no return, at the ascension to heaven ('...Touch me not, I have not yet been taken up to my Father..' says Christ to Mary of Magdala at the open tomb of Easter morning). He does come back from the Cross into this world and remains at the disposal of the suffering mankind, helping, consouling and compassioning men and helping them to find the way into the 'Pure Land'. This is nothing else but purest christian Gnosis, in the midst of the buddhist teachings and does turn it virtually into its contrary!

The results of the afore mentioned 4th Concilium at Srinagar in the year 78 post AD (Anno Domini), thus during the lifetime of Jesus in Cashmere, are reported to have been engraved on metal (copper?) plates or scrolls (similar to their famous counterparts of Qumran at the Dead Sea, written at the same period and found only in 1948 post), and are supposed to lie burried and concealed somewhere in the country. At that remote time, the spheres of influence of the two great buddhist schools, Hinayana and Mahayana, had been channeled for the future and for history: The Little Vehicle, Hinayana, the original doctrine of Buddhism, extended to the south, to Sri Lanka, Burma, Siam (Thailand), Indochina (Vietnam), and the Great Vehicle, Mahayana with its jesuanic doctrine of compassion in the wake, directed itself towards the north to conquer new areas for Buddhism, in Nepal, Tibet, Sinkiang, Mongolia, China, Corea and Japan.

This division does strangely remind us of the partition at Damascus between Christ and Paul, the East for the first, the West for the second. Should such metal plates one day appear at the light of the day, many a surprise could be expected. For instance, that the great saint of the valley of Cashmere, Yuz Asaph, hat participated in the name of his buddhist great king Kanishka at this Concilium that lasted half a year and that he did have a decisive part in its final results - and the schism of Buddhism.

*

30. The strange story of Nicolas Notovic - a fraud?

Orthodox Buddhism of the Little Vehicle, Hinayana, had, as is well known, abolished all the gods and divinities of Old India, together with social caste and human sacrifice, and had installed on the empty throne of god the 'Nexus Causalis', the law of origin and consequence, of 'action causing re-action'. This new doctrine developped during the 5th century BC (before Christ) in India, revealed itself als little comprehensive for the uneducated popular masses, but for the castes of the khsa trias, the classes of noble warriors, this enlightenment of the Guathama Buddha produced an excellent instrument for this second highest castes of India to break the domination of the arrogant priestly castes of brahmins that tyrannized the villagers and peasants in the country and banish their brahmanic cults of idolatry into the underground, where from that ancient system should gain supremacy again only after a thousand years in the great brahmanic counter-revolution against Buddhism and the restauration movement that laid the foundations of modern Hinduism. And Buddhism was then banished from its motherland, up to this day.

Is it possible, and imaginable, that the story of the drama of Golgotha in that remote land of Palestine and of the return of Jesus from the Cross where he had hoped to meet his heavenly Father, and back down to mankind, should have penetrated and reached listening ears in Cashmere? And should he, as a Perfect One who, from buddhist views, had managed to destroy his own kharma of re-births and who had, as a great saint, opened the tradition of the Bodhisattva-cult in Buddhism, should he, as the great teacher, entirely new for the Asian populations, have shown the way into the 'Pure Land' of the western paradise, to his Fathergod of boundless light, Abba? And should he have emerged in India to create for the first time the conception of compassion (where there has never been such a notion before in brahmanic dominated religion, nor in Hinayana Buddhism), and have given to the masses the hope to reach salvation by simple, unconditioned and fervent belief, without having to care constantly about the somber circle of reincarnation?

And if this had happened, how could the narration and tea-chings have reached remote India, if not through Jesus per-sonally -a f t e r- the completion of his flight out of Damascus, about 34 post, towards India which had lasted, altogether, nearly 14 years?

There does, in fact exist that strange story told by the wealthy Russian Nicolas Notovic who had undertaken, after the Crimean War in Russia, an extensive voyage to Central-Asia, to the Pamir, the roof of the world, and into north-west India, with the purpose of hunting bears and tigers. Around 1887 he reached, with numerous mules and indian porters to mountain valley of Cashmere, crossing over 13'000 feet high passes into Ladakh whose treeless and barren high mountain valleys are even to-day clad with a string of tibeto-buddhist monasteries. Therefore, Ladakh which continues to belong as its most northwesterly located area to the Indian Republic, had always also been known as 'Litte Tibet'.

In one of those monasteries, in Mulbeck, the traveller and big game hunter Notivic heard, by mere chance, by the abbot of the monastery the story of 'Saint Isa'. A great saint who had come in very remote times into Ladakh from a country in the far west and who had become one of the great teachers of Buddhism. Saint Isa would have left his land of birth on the western seashore at a young age with a commercial caravan and would have returned, in his later years, from the lands of Buddhism into his western fatherland in order to preach there the teaching of compassion, but that he had there been arrested, tortured, crucified (!) and brought to death. His memory would be kept in high esteem in Tibet, but only the most erudited and leading lamas (priests) would still have knowledge of his merits.

Notovic pointed his ears and recognized immediately in the figure of this buddhist saint our Lord, Jesus Christ. Following a counsel of the abbot, he moved further on into Ladakh and to the more important monastery of Hemis Gompa where, after considerable reluctance, old Tibetan scrolls, written in the holy Pali language, where indeed shown and red out to him. In these scriptures it was narrated that young Isa, or Issana, had left Philistea at the age of 13/14 years, had arrived in India, studied Brahmanism and Buddhism and would have returned at the age of some 30 years, in order to convert his nation to buddhist beliefs. But after a verdict by the Romans, he would have been hung, in the way of the Persians, to a Cross.

This appeared, indeed, to be a most sensational discovery, more so as Notovic realized that Jesus was in arabic called Isa, or Issana, and in persian Yuz. He returned to Europe with the respective translations, having everything carefully taken down on the spot, and published around 1908 in Paris a book in French, called: 'La deuxième vie de Jésus Christ' (The second life of Jesus Christ), - convinced, like at his time Columbus, to have entered new land and to have found the key-stone for the explenation of the missing period in Chrit's life between about 13-30 years. -Too good to be true?

But the edition of the booklet was hardly on the market, that it did already and mysteriously disappear, too early, and evidently bought up by unknown hands. This happened one hundred years ago. It will be interesting to see if, in the 21st century, christian society is still manipulated by similar irrational forces.

Meanwhile it has been established that the narration does really relate to Jesus Christ, but that incongruity is evident: Buddhist chroniclers of the first centuries had, quite obviously, converted Jesus of Nazareth into a buddhist who spread their teachings in Israel -what with absolute security had never been the case. How, however, could the story of the tragedy of Golgotha find its way into Tibetan chronics and annals? This became only possible if Christ had really appeared in India and related the events of Golgotha which nobody would otherwise know, personally. But Christ came to India -a f t e r- Calvary, and managed there to reform Buddhism, to become the very first Bodhisattva of the budd-hist faith in the pre-alpine countries of the Himalayas and was esteemed as a great teacher and saint, also in other buddhist countries.

But since buddhist self-pride would not admit for the generations to come that the great revolution of the buddhist faith, from the Hinayana to the new Mahayana doctrine, did come from outside, through a non-buddhist, the best solution to solve the problem was -to manipulate the truth into its contrary, for the glorification of the own religion.

What Nicolas Notovic did not find -and up to now, apparently, also nobody else-, is the continuation of the narrative of Saint Isa with the adventure of the migration of the Resurrected One to India a f t e r Golgotha. Such scriptures must have, un-doubtedly, existed, and therein might have been also told the exacter circumstances of Christ' s resurrection at Jerusalem, just as Christ might have told it himself in Cashmere in his own time. Perhaps. But such a second part of the narration would clearly defy the first part of it and demask it as a fraud. Or be it, his Excellency the Dalai Lama knew its hiding place and gave it one day free for publication, if he had an opportunity to do so, and if such a scripture did still exist, or had ever existed. In the interest of religious peace and the surprising discovery that Christianity and Mahayana Budd-hism ap-pear to have, at least in part, common roots, such a revelation would certainly be avoided by all means. There is very little doubt that the Vatican too does share the knowledge of this mystery.

It is noteworthy and a rather singular coincidence that Nicolas Notovic spent several weeks in the Cashmere capital city of Srinagar, at the very Dal Lake, without having the slightest clue of the so close genuine sepulchre of Christ; the latter would be re-discovered barely ten years after his departure. But this little mausoleum in the heart of Srinagar represents an enigmatic and neglected milestone of Christianity and does speak an eloquent language.

*

This, then, are -in a wider sense- the contents of a facts-book and resumé which does, maybe for the very first time, attempt to describe, honorify and, above all, explain the e n t i r e life of Jesus of Nazareth. Not only that small yet most important segment that has been known to christians for nearly two thousand years, but beginning some decades prior to his birth and ending some decades after his demise in the Cashmerian capital of Srinagar, India. In particular should the consequences of his existence be laid open and appreciated. It was nothing less than laying the foundations for the creation of an unseen spiritual, yet worldly empire that should take possession not only of the western hemisphere including the Americas, but also of large parts of Asia, comprehending even Japan. This edition on Christ will also trace the jesuanic ideas that did, quite visibly, influence and sublimate also Hinduism in the course of almost twenty centuries.

Numerous illustrations are at disposal. Amongst else also the genuine yet obscure and faded visage of Christ before his passion on the Cross, without injuries, as it could be reconstructed by means of computer-tomography in Italy and had been published there, on Easter 1985, as worldwide first release in the catholic magazine 'Christian Family'. This was, to say the least, a sensation. The Italian professor G. Tamburelli had made it possible, in two years' work with his team, to lift this great secret from the Holy Shroud of Christ guarded in Turin. This Shroud had at first been classified by the Vatican in 1988 as a falsification, but in the wake of vehement and worldwide protests by hundreds of scientists proving that the inherent chemical analysis had been an incredible fraud, the Vatican did publish a dementi and confirmed, once for ever, the genuinity of the Holy Shroud of Turin as Christ's original grave-cloth. We thus know to-day the appearance of the man who had come amongst us in charge of God Almighty to kindle a new light in this world, the flame of compassion, and what he had looked like. Whoever has seen that picture, then and to-day, would not forget it ever again. It does still visibly radiate the grandious teaching of Jesus, the 'Pater Noster', the spirit of the 'Sermon on the Mount', and the dispairing proclamation for a brotherly and peaceful co-existence and dramatic challenge of non-violence.

By the same author a publication-set of three books with a total of some 1600 pages is available (for the time being in german only), telling in the form of a dramatic narrative the principle events of the two lifes of Christ, in Palestine and in India, basing on all known historic facts up to now, be they of biblical sources of the New Testament, be they of non-christian sources. The title of this book-set reads:

'CHRIST - What at the Beginning was - and what happened after Calvary - The Epic Story' (CHRISTUS - Was am Anfang war - und was nach Golgatha geschah)

This narrative, positioned in the exotic and antique greco-roman world, and in an India at the dawn of its own history of two thousand years agao, may fascinate those who always desired to know more about the greatness of the enigmatic historical personality of Jesus Christ.

In the year 2008, another publication is foreseen, again at first in german language, of a historical and scientific character, of some 700 pages, with the title:

'CHRIST - The Truth - and the Proofs' (CHRISTUS - Wahrheit und Beweise)

These books comprehend and visualize the enormous material available on the life of Christ, known and unknown, and on his time, and were originally created with a view to the jubilee-year of Christianity 2000, and thought as a balance and review of what has been achieved, or not, in 20 long centuries of strife for a better world in the sense of its founder. Furthermore, the intention also is the motivation for a moderate reformation of to-days Christiandom, for a liberation of still to many pubertarian aspects, for correction of its errors and failures, and for the propagation of a model of elevated ethical thinking and intensified social justice, more respect to life of (all!) creatures, not only human and for the much stricter renounciation to violence. - And to slowly move away from the ambiguous events at the Empty Tomb of that remote Passah morning.

And, maybe, also to reveal and show, possibly, the nucleus of those corrections that appear to be the most urgent ones in order to preserve the venerable edifice of Chistianity from crumbling and to fortify, on the contrary, its very foundations to enable the mother-church to construct a second floor, for the foundation of

THE SECOND HOUSE OF CHRIST

for a new and more modern dignity and elevation of the teachings of its founder, but INSIDE the Holy Church, and not outside.

The PERCEPTION who Christ really was, and of his vision to erect down here on earth the Realm of Utopia, will slowly replace the simple beliefs - and make him, Christ, appear even greater than he has been hitherto in our minds.

Markus von Friedland
Author

Zurich, 1998, 2nd edition

—·—·—

31. What the consequences are: The stony way into the Second House of Christ

Our earthly existence is determined by the daily and trivial combat for survival that devours the lion's share of our energies. On our way through life we depend on spiritual guidance from above which, however, in spite of intense and continous search by mankindg, cannot be found. The only guidance that can perdure and outlast unstale governments fading ever away, are those of religious traditions and dogmatism, and those of philosophic treaties.

They illuminate our way with rites and light-house beams to which we can keep, that we can embrace, that offer consolation in phases of sorrow and distress, phenomena by which we are constantly hit anew, without ever being able to explain the origin of negative destinies.

Two of the great personalities of world history, Christ and Buddha, have shown us two ways to the land Utopia, to the realm of peace and to a more joyous and accomplished existence for all. Christ with his startling program of unconditioned protest against poverty and for the abolition of wars and violence with his commandment of brotherly co-existence. Buddha with his total renounciation on extrater-restial powers of gods and goddesses, his deliberate chal-lenge of the Ego in man, to political might, to avidity, to vanity, to unjustice, to jalousy and violence and his tremen-dous efforts for the creation of the new man of devotion, of mildness and contentment. Through domination and discip-lination of our emotions a large part of our self-caused sorrows and suffe-rings should be taken away from this world.

And while Buddhism did offer, since its very beginning, two levels of possible salvation -one for reaching higher forms of rebirth through kharmic improvement for the masses and lower population, and one to obtain the cracking of the circle of rebirths by annihilation of the proper kharma (ego) and thus final dissolution in Nirvana for the few-, christianity does know, right down to our days, but one exclusive level: The one of unconditioned belief and obedience according to the dogmata of the Ecclesia, or the canonic gospels for the protestant world. Whoever cannot embrace or accept this form of belief is no longer welcome in the great christian family.

In a highly technological and rapidly changing world which is coined by ultimate discoveries of science, the spectrum of christian churches has become too narrow and insufficient and cannot match anymore the religious exigences of large parts of christianity. Emancipated humans, men and women, have become reluctant to be pushed into a dark tunnel of obscure beliefs that do in no way correspond to the realities of modern life of our time. What would be necessary were a religious recipient that offers to millions of baptized christians the possibility to return into the folds of the christian com-munity, instead of turning their backs to the churches. This new recipient could be a SECOND HOUSE OF CHRIST that had to be built not outside, but inside of the Ecclesia, as an elevated story with a second floor where not so much beliefs would be required, but COGNIZANCE of the jesuanic, and perhaps also of the buddhist way to that remote realm of Utopia of an elevated mankind without suffering, misery, poverty, violence, wars and bloodshed that had once been promised to us by Jesus Christ. And which had, peremtorily and provisionally, been refused by the Father because the Son had opposed himself against the principles of creation that actually do include suffering and violence. Eventually, however, Christ's boundless compassion towards all creature proved stronger than God's reserve. With it, a new door had been pushed open to a way of a more joyous existence, less plastered with sorrow and liberated from primitive fears - if we only wished it!

But still we do not realize in full that the way must lead inwards, that we have to battle, dominate and conquer ourselves, in order to gain the prize of elevated and emancipated mankind. Victory over ourselves is greater than over the strongest opponent. The new altar of the Second House of Christ that will become possible only through correction of the historic foundations and beliefs of christianity, may lead us to an entirely new unity, insight and understanding and to victory over all our self-caused sufferings.

*

32. A Curriculum-warrant of Christ's life
CONTEMPORARY NOTES ON HIS EXTERNAL APPEARANCE:

There does exist a redescovered report of a probably political shadowing, probably from the years 29/30 post AD in Galilee, sent to Publius Lentulus, Roman super intendant of Pontius Pilate, stationed in Syria at that time, and reading:

> '...a man (Christ) of tall stature, 15,5 fists high
> (1,83 m), brown-red-blond hair, combed flat down
> to the ears, ondulated over the shoulders, wearing
> an exuberant beard parted in the middle, great,
> blue-greyish eyes, strange voice timber, strongly
> charismatic...'

and further reports:

'...mild in exhortations, tremendous when scolding, often good humoured and earnest, sometimes crying, but never see him laugh...'

and now furthermore at our disposition:

A computer-tomographic image by professor G. Tamburelli, Italy, with Christ's facial traits, condensed out of the Holy, genuine Shroud of Turin, with his team of scientists, whereby all injuries caused by tortures and from the crucifixion had been eliminated and correctioned, for example the broken nasal bone, the swollen right cheek, the wounds caused by the crown of thorns, the slaps in the face (see Christ's deadmask on the booklet-cover, published in the 'Christian-Family' magazine in Italy, as early as Easter 1985).

It's not the visage and expression of a hero, but a face full of compassion and misericordia -which, once seen- one does not easily forget and which could perfectly match the high spirit of the 'Sermon on the Mount'.

***

The way from an obvious and rough error to the truth is simple and straight, but from a refined and hidden error the way to the truth is tricky and painful - as it proves extremely difficult to unmask such mistakes.

Gotthold Ephraim Lessing

***

33. Life data of Jesus Christ:

Borne:	29th may	06 ante h	03.00 h ca at Bethlehem
Baptism in Jordan river	february	28 post h	at Jericho
Crucified;	03 april	32 post h	at Jerusalem
Ascension:	14th may	32 post h	Mount of Olives, Jerusalem (Luke)
Pentecost:	24th may	32 post h	M Zion,Jerusalem (Scha'wuoth)
Damascus:	october	33 post h	Encounter with Saulus/St.Paul
Traces:		34 post h	Nishibin (South-est Türkey)
Traces:		34 - 44 post h	Adiabene, Arbil, (North Iraq)
Traces:	48 post h		at Taxila (near Islamabad,Pak.)
Kashmer	78 post h		Cashmere Valley, Northwest India: Encounter with king Shale svahin, 4th Buddhist Concilium near Suryanagar (Srinagar)
Demise:	107 post h		at Srinagar, Kashmer, India, on shore of Dal Lake, at age 114

Ante h = BC, before Christ, historical count (h), at difference (a) astronomical count. 06 ante h = 07 ante a.

Post h = AD, Anno Domini, after Christ, historical count (h)

***

34. An Essay for an Astrological Evaluation:

Astrology is by no means an exact science, and it's status continues to be ranked with many a question mark. And this in spite of the fact that this primitive field of early studies has given birth to one of the most exact sciences: to Astronomy and the science of the Celestial bodies, their courses and their chemical compositions.

Since there is still many a thing between heaven and earth that is not measurable, it does certainly not mean a discrimination to a book of facts if we try to compare a hypothetical astrologic finding on Christ's life with the historical data so far known and ascertained to us, in order to see whether or not there are possible compliances which could further enlighten Christ's image to us. Even more so as two tousand years ago the zodiacal signs still kept their not too much earlier calculated positions in the sky in respect to the run of the sun, positions that differ to-day by about 30 days or one full zodiacal sign in comparison with the original Babylonian fixations -and our daily horoscopes do not in the slightest take such a remarkable difference in account!

And it is in fact astounding to find a quite obvious accordance between the astrological values and Christ's life data and characteristics as brought down to us by tradition, if we base and apply the above mentioned date of birth, and hour (+/- minutes):

Systems consulted:

Cortex, Huber: - Great conjunction Jupiter/Saturn in the
Zodiac of Fishes, 1st concourse,
07 ante, astronomical count (a)
29th may 07 ante, 03.00 hrs

Astrovisa 5,0:   - 06 ante, historical count (h)
29th may 06 ante, 03.00 hrs

In both cases the identical year and the
identical hypothetic hour of birth

The 1st concourse of the great conjunction of the planets Jupiter and Saturn of the year in question (out of three such passages in the same year, the following ones, however, visibles only for one night each), lastet from 24-29th May, year 06 (h)/07 (a), BC, ante (before Christ):

In the night 24-25th May, the moon stood near the great planet constellation, which meant unfavourable light conditions at the nightly sky and little eminence of the extraordinary light intensity emanated by the doubled onstellation of Jupiter and Saturn, standing side by side seen from Palestine.

In the night of the 28-29th May, however, the moon stood near the rising sun, which meant still considerably beneath the visible horizon at the time of birth at Bethlehem and thus the intense luminosity of the planet constellation was very promi-nent in the dark and undisturbed nightly sky over Bethlehem - the age of electric light was still 2000 years away.

**

Zodiac sign	GEMINI	Birth at Bethlehem, 29.05.06 ante (historical count) hour 03.00 h in the night
Ascendant	ARIETE	In the case of birth, coordinates values for Bethlehem, hours 02.14-03.06 h, night 28/29th May
	TAURUS	In the case of birth, coordinates values for Bethlehem, hours 03.07-04.17 h, night 28/29th May

**

Character	Two faces:	like god Janus of ancient Rome
	Two aspects:	having two souls in ones breast

Strong inclination to social justice, sharp intelligence, great talents for organisation, managment for stage plays, theatre, dramaturgic line, leadership, sense of responsibility

Twin-sign bornes (Gemini) often seek harmony through conflicts; in the case of Christ: rage, hard-wordy ammonitions,
mildness, compassion, tears (Toro-sign inflfuence?)

Sturdy persecution of a once set goal, unsverwing (Ariete-
sign influence?)

*

HOROSCOPE: Stand of planets at birth:

SUN   The sun's position at the initial sector
of Gemini (Twins): underlined EGO
aspect, great self-consciousness, in-
transparent for others, can easily stay
alone in life

MERCURY, 3rd House
Communication of throughts, pro-
nounced teacher-ship

Most planets stand in the EGO-section,
but

PLUTO   Creative power, YOU-aspect, axis
Fishes-Virgo: assistance, help, healing,
social engagement, fortified through

MARS   plus Leo-Virgo, 5th House,
motoric effects

NEPTUN   Extremely YOU-side related, unselfish
love, strong intuition for others' feelings
spiritual emancipation (foggy-shing too)
Consciousness enlarging substances
for consumation imaginable

URANUS   11th House:
Equally minded, spiritual friends

GEMINI   Interests in multiple matters, but short-
timed and quickly saturated, many
changes, also superficial

TRIANGULUM (red) of Efficiency:

> Enormously dynamic and perpetual
> motion (almost continous migration in
> the case of Christ in many phaes of his
> life.
>
> *

A Horoscope disk does stand for 72 years of life; then
everything does start anew, as a repetition of the very same
constellations. If we do observe the life of Christ, as far as we
can now reconstruct it, according to age phases and correlation to the time periods, we are struck by the strange accordance with his horoscope features above exposed:

AGE	CURRICULUM VITAE	EPOCH
01-16 years	Strong planetary constellations, years of intense learning, self-consciousness, awakening	06 ante - 10 post
16-26	Relatively void, tranquillity	10 post - 20 post
27-36	Inner recollection and preparation	21 post - 28 post
37-39 years	Public mission and agitation, extremely active	28 post - 31 post
39	Drama on Golgotha With 38/39 years passing under Neptun in his horoscope. Period of culmination Maximum maturity, Halftime of the horoscope-life, Retrospective, Uncertainty.	32 post
39-62 years	Void of planetary constellations, few events, rather passive phase, years of flight	33 post - 55 post
63-72	Yuz Asaph (Jesus Christ) in Kashmer. In 54 post he becomes active at the temple of the throne of Salomon at Srinagar, India, and declares	56 post - 65 post

his profethical office as a son of
the Bani (Children) Israel. This does
concord with the position of
Uranus in the 11th House: 56 post - 65 post
Acceptance of new spiritual obliga-
tions and challenges. Again we have
the Jupiter/Saturn constellation in his
horoscope as at the time of birth. Strong
impulses, migratory activities and mission
in India and the Himalayan countries

72-90   Repetition of the constellation of   66 post - 84 post
years: his youth with Sun, Moon, Mercury,
Venus. Important events take place:
in 78 post encounter with king Raja
Shalesvahin in Kashmer, possible par-
ticipation in the 4th Buddhis Concilium
at Haran/Srinagar. Again the Red Triangulum of extraordinary efficiency (Jupiter
and Saturn in the zodiac of Fishes, in the
12th Hosue. Culmination again of social
engagement and

90-114   again under Pluto, Axis Pisces-Virgo,
years: in the 12th House, with Mars as   84 post-107 post+
motoring unit. Unheard manifestation
of mutual aid, assistance, and great
compassion even more accentuated
during his very last years, selfless
brotherly love and misericordial emotions.

**

The result of this hypothetical examination:

The horoscope of Jesus of Nazareth could indeed confirm the supposition that:

YUZ ASAPH (CHRIST) became in Kashmer, India, the Divine Compassionate and advanced to the Buddhist Divinity of Boundless Mercy AVALOKITHESVARA (in Sanskrit language), founding the great Bodhisattva-cult in the reformed buddhist religion, in the 1st century of our (his) time, exactly in the north-west corner of India, and with it the buddhist Mahayana school of the 'Great Vehicle'.

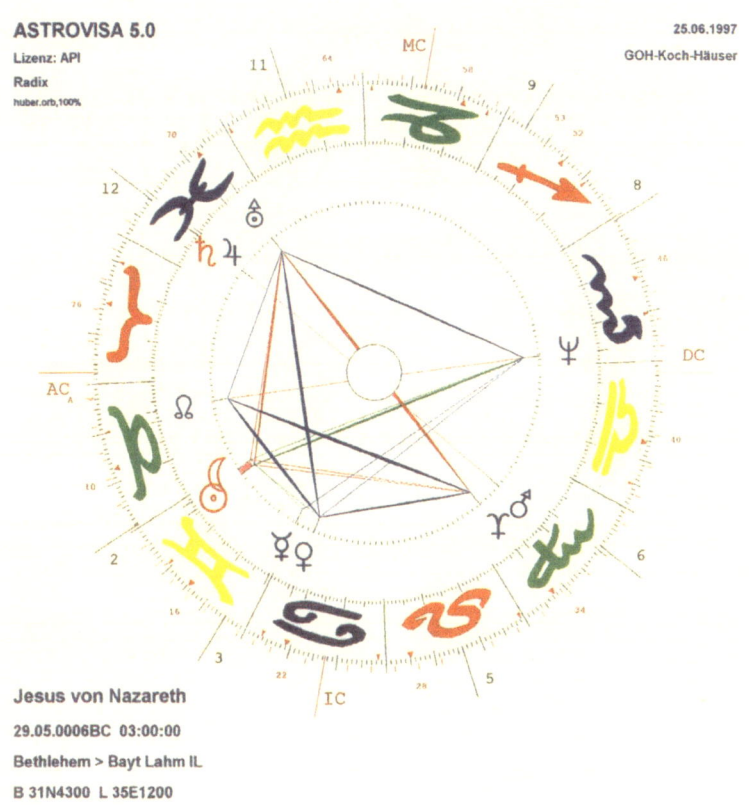

ASTROVISA 5.0

Lizenz: API

Radix

huber.orb,100%

25.06.1997

GOH-Koch-Häuser

Jesus von Nazareth

29.05.0006BC 03:00:00

Bethlehem > Bayt Lahm IL

B 31N4300 L 35E1200

The Mausoleum (Rauzabal) of the prophet Yuz Asaph (alias Jesus Christ) in Khanyar-Street, at Srinagar-city, Kashmer, India, situated in a muslim quarter (three arches = north side)

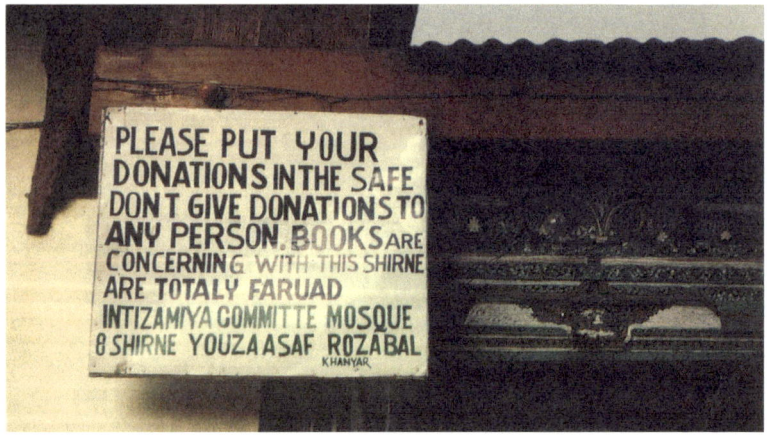

A new panel at the sepulchre of Yuz Asaph, photographed in 1988. Very interesting the phrase: 'Books are concerning with this shrine are totaly faruad (fake)..., applied by the Muslim curatorium of the suburb. - What does an old proverb say? Where there is smoke, the fire is not far...

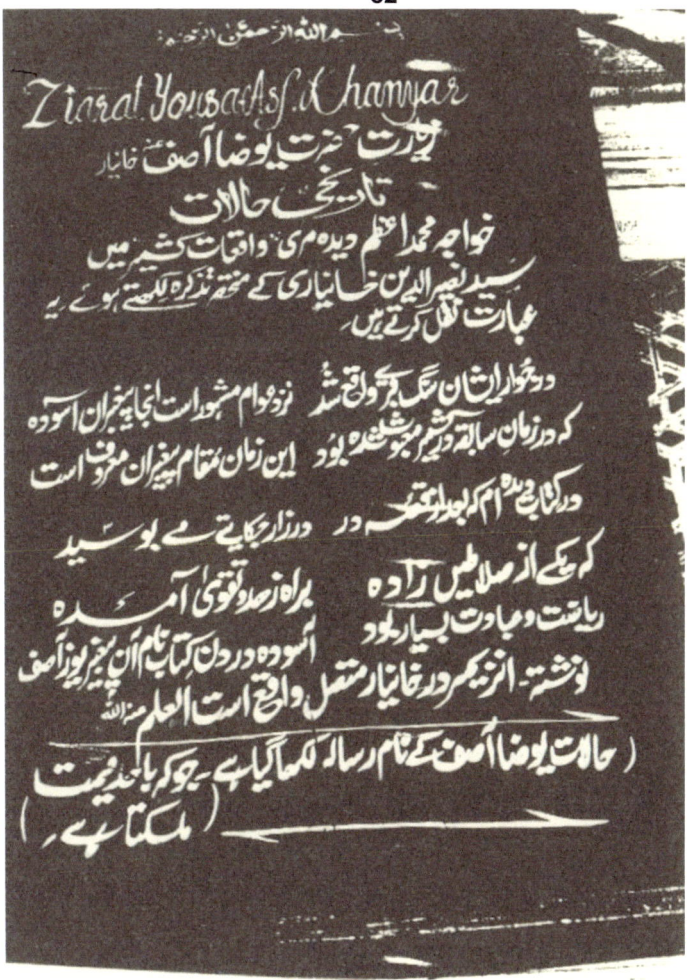

The old panel at the Rauzabal, in arab writing and persian language (earlier the official administrative language in north-west India) which relates that in occasion of the re-discovery of this tomb after the Muslim invasion of Kashmer in the 14th century a muddy old writing had been found in the grave chamber that was almost entirely destroyed yet mentioned that it were the sepulchre of a great prophet of fair skin in times of antiquity who had come, many hundreds of years ago, in the valley of Kashmer to preach God and conduct a holy life.

The enigmatic sepulchral Mausoleum of the great, unknown prophet Yuz Asaph (Jesus Christ?) in Khanyar-Street, Srinagar, Kashmer (5 arches = east side)

A photograph of Professor F.M. Hassnain, Srinagar, in his house dress, at his home, who had re-descovered the tomb of Yuz Asaph around 1985, in his own city, together with the autor, Markus von Friedland

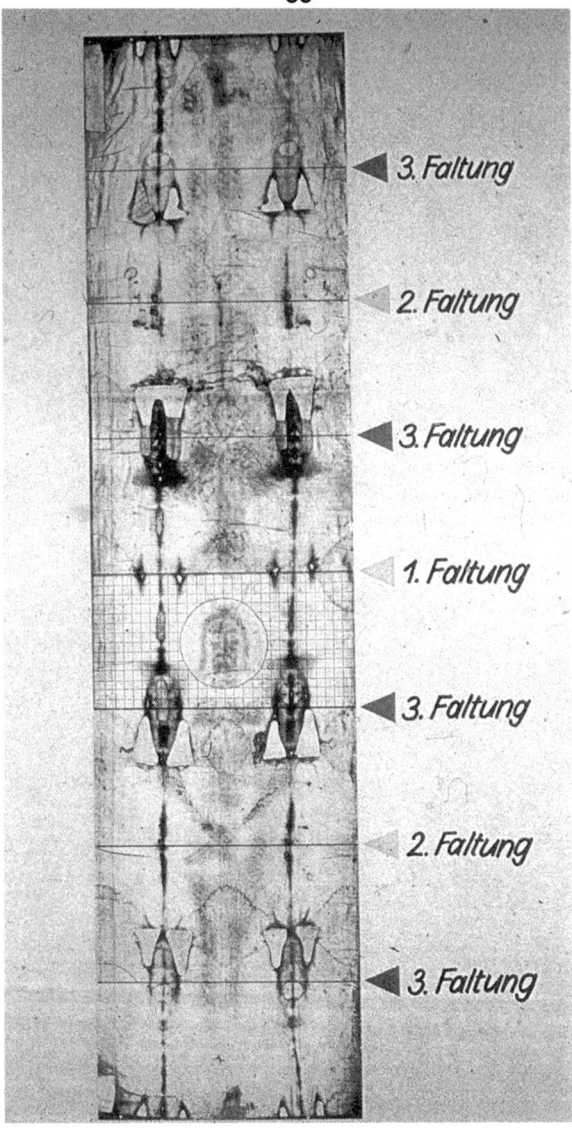

The photo-negative print of Christ's body, in the double-fol-
ded, genuine Holy Shroud (The Linen) in Turin of nearly two
thousand years ago, first photographed and discovered by the
Italian photographer Secondo Pia, in 1898, in Turin

The magnificent painting of Christ's crucifixion by El Greco, Spain, end of 16th century, in the El Prado musum, Madrid

***

German edition:
Zurich, December 1999

English edition:
Zurich, June 2006   Markus von Friedland
                                                  Author, Dr.h.c.

Christ

MARKUS von FRIEDLAND

What you are holding in your hand, Dear Reader, is NOT an easy flowing and harmless narrative, no adventure story, no heroic epos, no portrait, no biography or literary essay. Neither is it a documentary report nor a theatre piece or an esoteric tale.

What is it then? – It is nothing less than the tragic and unique history of the TWO LIVES of one of the greatest personalities who ever wandered on this earth, of the man from Nazareth who would change part of this world profoundly.
– Two Lives ?? –

It was a merely accidental encounter with young students in the remote Mexico that brought the author on the trace of a strange legend out of West-Tibet, today the Indian province of Ladakh. According to which the young Jesus of Nazareth had spent his silent years of formation in the far away country of India.

An unusual story thus became the trigger for the creation of two literary works that led, after thorough investigation in Palestine, Kashmir and Ladakh to a sensational new interpretation of the extremely eventful, movimentated and particularly long life of Christ. The author, Markus von Friedland, borne 1930 in Wil, St. Gall, Switzerland, from and to Toggenburg and Neuenburg, did, after his studies and a life-long activity in the domaine of international Tourism and as a professor at renomated faculties of Tourism, consecrate twenty years of his leisure time to the writing of a dramatic narrative of the Two Lives of Jesus, in three volumes, and a special book on the theme, the 'Book of Truth and Proofs'.

May many readers draw pleasure and mental impulse from the lecture, and motivation to help constructing, actively and spiritually, the Second House of Christ, inside and not outside of the Mother Church, in order to find, one remote day, the promised Land of Utopia.

In occasion of the 25th World Congress of the World Development Parliament in Delhi, India (Vishwa Unnyayan Samsad) of 12th March 1988, the author was honoured with the title of a Dr. h.c. (honoris causa) for his intense researches and merits in the field of modern and historically founded Christology.

The epic tale of Christ, and on how it all begann and what happened at and after Crucifixion and his survival at the Cross, comes in three fascinating volumes, tracing step by step the dramatic events in his life, all clad in the glamour and the brutality of the antique Mediterranean world. We accompany Christ on his desperate mission in judaic Palestine, see him encounter Paul at Damascus and wander away out of the New Testament and the Bible, to the East, to arrive in the year 48 post of his own calendar counting(!) at Taxila in Northern India, at the court of king Gondaphor, possibly one of the Three Magoi Kings of Bethlehem, in his birth-year. And we realize with astonishment that he achieves to reform Buddhism, and make it a great relilgious movement, greater than before. He died a natural death at 114 years of age at Srinagar, Kashmir, India.

The 'Book of Truth and Proofs' eventually unveils the great secret of the Nazarene who saw himself as the Epiphany of his Fathergood in the Heavens, for wom he founded the Unseen Kingdom of the Hearts on this earth. He was crucified as the real heir to the throne of Israel, out of the Hasmonean Dynasty and the House of David, by adoption. From the Sacred Shroud of Turin it is definitely accepted that he survived crucifixion and led a second life among us with unheard success, also in the East. Time has come to acknowledge the historical facts for the sake of truth – that was so particularly dear to him.

Herstellung und Verlag: Books on Demand GmbH, Norderstedt
ISBN: 978-3-8334-7762-1